Shashi Tharoor's

The Great Indian Novel

A Critical Study

Celebrating Indian Literature

Shashi Tharoor's

The Great Indian Novel

A Critical Study

Tapan K. Ghosh

abc
asia book club
an international publishing house

Published by
Asia Book Club
C 3/1, Janakpuri
New Delhi 110 058
Ph. 25507139, 9818755529
email: prestigebooks@gmail.com
website: www.asiabookclub.com
ISBN: 81-7851-31-6

Printed at Chaman Offset Press, New Delhi 110 002

Contents

Additional Criticism: What Others Say

Preface

A diplomat-turned-writer, Shashi Tharoor is a name to reckon with in contemporary Indian writing in English. His literary oeuvre is small but it is remarkable for its seriousness of intent and solidity of substance. Through his fiction and non-fiction works, this highly placed UN official, who views writing as a process of self-discovery, has affirmed the Indian cultural identity by reflecting on its multiplicity and syncretism and broadened our understanding of the country's great heritage.

The Great Indian Novel, Tharoor's first novel, is a literary landmark. Published to great critical acclaim in 1989, the book won two major awards and put its author in the front rank of Indian English writers. The novel is a political satire which reinterprets the major strands of the 20th century Indian history in the form of an epic spoof. In Tharoor's ambitious and eloquent retelling, the story of modern India is transformed into the ancient epic, the *Mahabharata*. The book ingeniously combines past and present, history and myth, parody and polemic, politics and philosophy, prose and verse, reckless humour and hard-hitting satire to present a poignant saga of the great subcontinent.

The present book is a serious attempt to examine this outstanding novel from critical perspectives. It begins with a brief overview of Shashi Tharoor's life and works and a general introduction to the text of *The Great Indian Novel*. This is followed by exploratory essays on the novel by eminent scholars that offer a wide spectrum of views on the author and the text.

I am indebted to Dr. R.K. Dhawan who inspired me to write the book. My friends Dr. Harideb Sil and Prof. Shyamlal Sukul and my nephew Sourav Kumar helped me immensely to prepare the manuscript. I take this opportunity to acknowledge my debt of gratitude to them and to the scholars who have contributed well-researched articles to this book. While the first contributor Dr. Sudhendu Shekhar is a perceptive critic of Shashi Tharoor, the second contributor, a French scholar and critic, Ludmila Volná, an ardent admirer of India, has done commendable research work on Indian English literature.

My wife Sipra has been very supportive throughout the entire process. To her, as to my mother who has always refreshed my memory about the stories of the *Mahabharata*, my debt is immeasurable.

TAPAN KUMAR GHOSH

Introduction
Shashi Tharoor: His Life and Works

Shashi Tharoor appeared on the literary scene in 1989 with his first work of fiction, *The Great Indian Novel*, and established himself in the front rank of contemporary Indian writers in English. The book won two major literary awards[1] and was highly acclaimed by critics in India and abroad.

A diplomat and writer, Shashi Tharoor was born in 1956 in London and educated in Bombay, Calcutta, Delhi and the United States. After graduating from St. Stephen's College (Delhi), he completed his Ph.D. from Fletcher School of Law and Diplomacy at Tufts University (U.S.A.) at the age of 22. In 1976, while he was still a student, Tharoor won the Rajika Kripalani Young Journalist Award for Indian journalists under the age group of thirty. Since May 1978, Tharoor has worked for the United Nations, at first with the UN High Commissioner for Refugees in Geneva and Singapore and later with the UN Headquarters in New York. Between 1989 and 1996, he served as Special Assistant to the Under-Secretary General for Peace-keeping operations. In this capacity, he addressed a variety of peace-keeping issues around the world and led the UN team for peace-keeping operations in former Yugoslavia. In 1997, Tharoor was appointed Executive Assistant to the Secretary General of the United Nations, Kofi Annan, and in 2006 he was declared India's candidate for the top post of this international organization.

In spite of holding responsible positions in professional life, Tharoor has successfully combined two different vocations—diplomacy and writing. As an author, he has written many editorials, commentaries and short stories in Indian and Western publications. His first published book, *Reasons of State* (1982), is a scholarly and highly praised study of India's foreign-policy making. *The Great Indian Novel*, Tharoor's first fictional work, was published in 1989. The novel is a political satire which interprets, with flamboyant style and uncommon fluency, the *Mahabharata* as India's modern history from the country's struggle against British Raj to the Emergency and its aftermath. The interpretation of reality through myth and history often results in thinly veiled caricatures of well-known characters and situations from the epic and politics. But Tharoor's avowed aim in this novel is to affirm Indian cultural identity by highlighting its pluralism and openness. *The Great Indian Novel* is a spirited acknowledgement, and a bold assertion, of 'the multiplicity of truth that has given shape and substance to the idea of India.'[2]

His second work of fiction, *The Five Dollar Smile*—a collection of short stories and a play—was published in 1990. Most of the stories were written when Tharoor was in his late teens and early twenties. With the exception of 'Solitude of the Short-Story Writer,' the stories are set in India and they deal with cosmopolitan city-dwellers who, in spite of being increasingly seduced by western culture, still retain an emotional attachment for the countryside they had left long ago. The most moving piece in the anthology is, of course, the title story in which a lonely orphan, who is used as the poster child of an organization that raises money for the purpose of charity, is determined to visit the family in America that have adopted him. He writes to them touching letters about his ambition which result in an air-ticket for a three-week visit to the U.S.A. But during the flight, the boy—surrounded by strangers—experiences a bout of intense and inexplicable loneliness that leaves him completely dispirited. By turn funny and touching, the stories also deal with the trauma of youth as well as death, deceit, hypocrisy and the conflict of cultural change.

Tharoor's second novel, *Show Business*, is a pungent satire on the Bombay film industry, which came out in 1992. The book was subsequently adapted into a motion picture called *Bollywood*. The narrative follows the career of a famous film-star Ashok Banjara, from the period when the struggling actor tried to find a foothold in the film world to the time when he fought for survival after a fatal accident in a shooting zone. The character of Banjara is modelled on Amitabh Bachchan whose life closely parallels that of the fictional hero. As a backdrop to Banjara's rise to the acme of Bombay's commercial cinema is a non-stop carousel of the major blockbusters he has acted in—'a never ending fantasy that took over his life completely and transformed it into an astonishing, though compelling, lie.'[3] Tharoor uses film, which he considers to be an important medium for transmitting fictional experience to the Indian masses, as a creative metaphor to explore the contemporary myths which are invented by the popular Hindi cinema and, through them, certain aspects of Indian life. Though a montage of narrative, shooting scripts, songs and monologues, he invents a fictional world that becomes an expressive metaphor for deeper truths: illusion and reality, ambition and greed, love, deception and death. His fifth book, *India: From Midnight to the Millennium*, was published in 1997. Written to commemorate the 50th anniversary of India's Independence, the book examines what the emancipation from colonial rule meant for the country, providing in the process a perceptive analysis of her past, present and future. Tharoor combines elements of political scholarship, personal reflection, polemic, memoir and fiction in the book which deals with a wide range of subjects including India's rich cultural heritage, her contribution to the western world, the strength of Indian democracy as well as the country's economic reforms, caste system and governmental corruption.

His third novel *Riot* was published to much critical acclaim in 2001. A vibrant work of fiction about the communal flare-up in northern India in the wake of *Ram Janambhumi* movement by Hindu extremists in late 1980s and early 1990s, the book takes on a wide range of topics. On one level, Tharoor examines the reasons of communal tension between Hindus and Muslims through the postmortem of a fictional riot. He engages with this palpable tension with much insight, offering in the process a balanced critique of both Hindu cultural nationalism and Muslim fundamentalism, and a convincing account of the role of the administration in controlling riots. On another level, the book is concerned with unravelling the mystery that surrounds the murder of an idealistic American student and welfare worker, Priscilla Hart, who comes to India to volunteer in a women's health programme, during the riot. The novel, highly praised for its brilliant experimentation with narrative form, chronicles the unresolved mystery of Priscilla Hart's death through the mutually contradictory accounts of a group of characters who narrate their individual versions of the events which led to the tragedy. Intellectually challenging and emotionally engrossing, *Riot* is a fictional tour-de-force 'about the ownership of history, about love, hate, cultural collision, religious fanaticism, and the impossibility of knowing the truth.'[4]

Tharoor's latest work, *Bookless in Baghdad* was published in 2005. It is a collection of book reviews, literary musings, and columns on writers like Naipaul, Rushdie, Kipling and Wodehouse. Apart from perceptive and highly readable essays like 'Mining the Mahabharata,' 'Bhartiya Sanskrit in the Big Apple' and 'The Cultural Geography of Criticism,' the anthology contains personalized self-commentary on the condition of a literary exile, an Indian author abroad who is adrift in an ocean of western culture.

Shashi Tharoor takes his vocation as a writer very seriously. Writing is a process of self-discovery for him. He admits in an interview with *The Asian Age*[5] that he has 'a number of responsibilities' which he seeks to express through his writings. He said to the interviewer: "I explore things that matter to me, like our Indian heritage, the forces that are making and unmaking India and also the dilemmas, problems and situations we are dealing with in our society and civilization." Through his novels and non-fiction works, Tharoor has affirmed the Indian cultural identity by reflecting on its multiplicity and syncretism and broadened our understanding of the country's great heritage. Rejecting the unitary narrative of Indian myth, history and culture, he has boldly asserted that there is more than one Indian culture and, more importantly, more than one view of Indian culture. Through his variegated writings this diplomat-turned-author has underscored the cultural diversity of India and explored the themes of the country's past and its relevance to the future.

NOTES

1. The FIP—Hindustan Times Literary Award (1989-90) and the Commonwealth Writers Prize (1990).
2. Shashi Tharoor, 'Yoking of Myth to History,' *Littcrit*, Vol. 16, Nos. 1+2 (June-December, 1990), p. 8.
3. Blurb
4. See the blurb
5. November 15, 2005.

The Great Indian Novel: A Critical Evaluation

The Great Indian Novel derives its title not from the author's assessment of the book's content but 'in deference to its primary source of inspiration, the ancient epic the *Mahabharata*.'[1] Shashi Tharoor has taken the *Mahabharata* as a blueprint and filled it with a contemporary cast for his witty send-up of pre- and post-independence India. Like Salman Rushdie, he has re-constructed the major strands of modern Indian history in the form of an epic spoof. The history of India's struggle against colonial rule and her postcolonial tryst with democracy is presented in an epic vein. Like the epic of Vyasa, the novel is divided into eighteen books and its narrative is presented in a variegated style and a digressive manner. The historical narrative follows the line of the *Mahabharata* providing insight both into current politics and into the epic.

Tharoor uses an allegorical mode in which the ancient epic becomes a structuring device to create a highly individual version of Indian history. As the narrator, Ved Vyas, says to his elephant-headed amanuensis, Ganapathi, at the end of the introductory chapter: "This is my story, the story of Ved Vyas" (18).[2] Ved Vyas, a cantankerous and old politician, tells his story, which he calls 'the definitive memoir of [his] life and times' (18), to his scribe Ganapathi who functions both as an implied reader within the text and a continuous reminder of the present tense of the narrating time.

The entire narrative is dictated by the octogenarian participant-narrator from his falling memory to Ganapathi. This adds a distinct tone of orality to the novel. Ved Vyas's orally transmitted tale seeks not only to supplant the recorded British history of colonized India with a counter discourse but also to undermine and subvert the hagiographic account of some leaders like Nehru, Indira, and Jayaprakash Narayan in post-independence India. He stresses the subjective nature of his 'memoir' or 'memory's truth' (in Rushdie's famous formulation) which has been prompted by a need to correct the notion held abroad that India is an 'underdeveloped country' and to show that she is, in fact, 'a highly developed [country] in an advanced state of decay' (17). That is why he wants his account, which is full of irreverent playfulness, to be taken as seriously as the *Mahabharata* itself: "We're not writing a piddling western thriller here. This is my story, the story of Ved Vyas, eighty-eight years old and full of irrelevancies, but it could become nothing less than *The Great Indian Novel*" (18).

While Ved Vyas, like Saleem Sinai in Salman Rushdie's *Midnight's Children*, insists on presenting a subjective interpretation of the collective experience, Shashi Tharoor declares his intention to speak 'for an India of multiple realities and multiple interpretation of reality. Throughout the novel runs an acknowledgement of the multiplicity of truth that has given shape and substance to the idea of India.'[3] This assertion of the 'multiplicity of truth' and 'multiple interpretation of reality' brings Tharoor's novel very close to Rushdie's canonical text with which it has been, very justifiably, compared.

NOTES

1. The author's note on the title in the beginning of the novel.
2. Shashi Tharoor, *The Great Indian Novel* (New Delhi: Penguin Books, 1989).
3. 'Yoking of Myth to History,' p. 8.

The Great Indian Novel and *Midnight's Children:* A Study in Comparison

Tharoor evinces an anxiety of influence by making an explicit reference to *Midnight's Children* in his novel. One of the chapters of *The Great Indian Novel* is entitled 'Midnight's Parents.' Again, while cataloguing the immediate changes which occurred in national life after the attainment of independence, Ved Vyas says: "Children being born at inconvenient times of the night who would go on to label a generation and rejuvenate a literature" (239).

There are a number of thematic similarities between *Midnight's Children* and Tharoor's novel. Both the books narrate the history of the nation through the story of a family. They cover almost the same period of Indian history and highlight some key incidents like the Jallianwala Bagh massacre, the partition of India, the murder of Gandhi, the wars with Pakistan and China, the conquest of Goa, the dismemberment of Pakistan and the birth of Bangladesh, the declaration of Emergency and its aftermath. While *Midnight's Children* is a novel about 'broken promises,' *The Great Indian Novel* is about the 'betrayed expectations' of the people. Both are memory novels which use orality as the mode of narration.

Like Rushdie, Tharoor presents 'memory's truth' and foregrounds memory as an inextricable part of his delineation of India. His book also affirms the importance of memory in the reclamation of personal and collective history. Both the authors try to achieve an animating correspondence between the past and the present and use a hybrid mode of narration that dexterously combines myth and history, autobiography and fiction, dream and fantasy, prose and verse. One finds in their novels an interplay between contemporary Indian reality and its mythical parallel. In *Midnight's Children* myth functions as a kind of shorthand to convey concepts; it is not elaborately worked out as in *The Great Indian Novel* which employs myth as a framework. While Rushdie manipulates the myth of the 'midnight's children' to present his version of India's postcolonial history, Tharoor transforms the ancient myth of the country into her pre- and post-Independence politics. But both the authors assume a parodic stance towards their mythic material. Their use of myth in their respective novels is playful and ironic in the postmodernist manner.

Tharoor presents the history of modern India from the point of view of an individual. He seems to suggest, like Rushdie, that subjective reclamation of the past provides a version of truth which is valid for the individual. As his narrator, Ved Vyas, says: "It is my truth, Ganapathi, just as the crusade to drive out the British reflected Gangaji's truth, and the fight to be rid of both the British and the Hindu was Karna's truth" (104). Tharoor writes, very much like the creator of *Midnight's Children*, a subversive history which destabilizes the certainty of the official version.

In spite of such thematic correspondences, the two novels differ in their narratological intents. The difference lies in the replacement of fantasy, which informs Rushdie's book, by an elaborate structure of myth in Tharoor's novel. Moreover, the narrator's attitude in *The Great Indian Novel* is that of an ironic observer; he has no emotional involvement in the experiences of the nation. Therefore, his story that combines parody with polemic, does not emotionally involve the readers. The anguish and bewilderment that Saleem Sinai feels as he, like his nation, gets buffeted by the inexorable forces of history, are not to be found in Tharoor's novel which, though more politically engaged than Rushdie's work, strikes an impersonal note.

The Great Indian Novel as Allegorical Representation of History

The novel's title, a literal translation of the *Mahabharata*, links it to the great epic of Vyasa. In the 'Afterword' to the novel, Tharoor writes, "Many of the characters, incidents and issues in the novel are based on the people and events described in the great epic the *Mahabharata*, a work which remains a perennial source of delight and inspiration to millions in India" (419). In another essay entitled 'Myth, History and Fiction,'[1] he states more explicitly that *The Great Indian Novel* is 'an attempt to retell the political history of 20th century India through a fictional recasting of events, episodes and characters from the *Mahabharata*.' This is tantamount to admitting that the novel, which contains Tharoor's version of the political history of modern India, is modelled on the ancient epic in terms of structure, issues and characters. The statement also confirms the fact that (a) the shape and the sequential movement of the novel are dictated by the epic and (b) Tharoor's fictional work is predetermined by a meta-text which is already familiar to his readers.

The allegorical representation of recent history through the epic narrative provides Tharoor with a number of advantages. The *Mahabharata* is a foundational text of Indian literature and an inextricable part of its living tradition. Any work of fiction that is modelled on it would naturally be assured of a general acceptability and an interest among its readers.

Secondly, despite its mythological background, the epic has a considerable historical core and it embraces virtually all the vital aspects of human experience. This makes it an appropriate model for a fictional reconstruction of national history. The *Ma-*

habharata is also an imitable text for writing any historical narrative which centers around such themes as power, politics, conspiracy, clash of personalities, institutional structures and individual as well as collective dharma. These thematic concerns are also to be found at the centre of Tharoor's reconstruction of modern Indian history.

Thirdly, the *Mahabharata*, which is generally attributed to Vyasa, does not have any fixed text and is believed to have been re-written time and again. As such the epic affords a good deal of flexibility and freedom to an author who intends to use it as a paradigm. Tharoor thus enjoys the freedom to write his own version of the epic. *The Great Indian Novel* is actually the *Mahabharata* re-written from the postcolonial as well as postmodernist perspectives. Finally, the multifarious texture of the epic with its loose, episodic structure gave Tharoor another fi eedom, that of using a varied range of styles in his novel. He exploits this stylistic variety to great artistic effect. *The Great Indian Novel* is a sprawling narrative which attempts to present the recent history of India in a parodic vein. Tharoor's avowed purpose in the book is to 'throw certain trends and issues into sharper relief than history makes possible.'[2] To achieve this objective, he employs several forms of irreverent style like puns, wordplay, irony, sarcasm, light verse, jokes and humorous digressions. Through the deployment of stylistic diversity Tharoor seeks to approximate another significant aspect of the epic which is highlighted by Shyamala Narayan in an essay entitled "Verbal Pyrotechnics: A Note on *The Great Indian Novel*": "The story of India, like that of *Mahabharata*, had to come across as a tale of many tellers, even if it is ascribed only to one."[3]

What serves as the springboard of the allegorical scheme in the novel is the idea that the battle of Kurukshetra, the paradigmatic struggle between good and evil, virtue and vice, *dharma* and *adharma*, never ends. As Ved Vyas, the modern prototype of the epic narrator, asserts: "History is Kurukshetra. The struggle between *dharma* and *adharma* is a struggle of our nation, and each of us in it, engages in on every single day of our existence. That struggle, that battle took place before . . . ; it will continue"

(391). According to Tharoor, the political history of twentieth century India closely resembles, and can be properly understood only in relation to, the events and the characters of the *Mahabharata*. The ancient epic provides for his novel the appropriate allegorical background to project the modern Indian situation. He uses the mythical narrative to foreground the continuity of the historical process from the remote past to the immediate present: "in my epic I shall tell of past, present and future, of existence and passing, of efflorescence and decay, of death and rebirth; of what is, of what was, of what should have been" (18).

The battle of Kurukshetra is also an occasion for the restoration of values and the upholding of truth and dharma. The historic struggle of the Indian people for freedom from British rule was one such battle. Again, the issue of sharing the Kingdom of Hastinapur pitted the Pandavas and the Kauravas against each other and resulted in the fratricidal battle. Similarly, the question of sharing the fruits of power determined the course of the country's post-independence history, and ultimately led to the degeneration of democratic values and the declaration of Emergency. The story of values like truth and/or dharma being deserted for selfish and parochial ends and the consequent chaos in national life informs the text of both the *Mahabharata* and *The Great Indian Novel*.

Through a severe indictment of the postcolonial Indian politics, the novelist seeks to arrive at a binarism: the chaos versus the truth and dharma. The novel shows that contemporary India has been transformed into a 'muddle' by her self-serving and tunnel-visioned politicians, the modern prototypes of the ancient Kauravas, who destroyed the glorious tradition of the country represented by Bhishma in the epic and Gandhi in the recent past. It thus makes a daring and innovative use of the epic story for interpreting the historical process and uses the allegorical mode for making a trenchant criticism of the political history and personalities of the twentieth century India.

What *The Great Indian Novel* attempts to underscore is the continuity of the historical process. It demonstrates that even though the great epic warriors had died on India's mythological battlefields long ago, epic battles have been fought for great causes like freedom and restoration of democracy in the modern history of the country. The national movement for freedom from colonial rule and the people's uprising against Indira Gandhi's dictatorial regime mark the continuation of the epic struggle between *dharma* and *adharma* fought on the battleground of Kurukshetra. Viewed from this perspective, the recent history of India is a reflection of what happened in the *Mahabharata*. The simultaneity of the epic and the contemporary history, of tradition and modernity, is further suggested by the fact that instead of using two separate time frames for the mythic age and the modern, Tharoor inextricably fuses them into one, presenting characters and events from the *Mahabharata* as contemporaneous with the present age.

Embodied in the past, the characters feel and act in the present. Thus, Ganga Datta, going to meet Satyavati's father in the forest and ask her hand for his own father Shantanu, is described as both *Gangaputra* Bhishma and Mohandas Karamchand Gandhi:

> Ganga Datta didn't travel alone either. In later years he would be accompanied by a non-violent army of *satyagrahis*, so that the third-class train carriages he always insisted on travelling in were filled with the elegantly sacrificing elite of his followers, rather than the sweat-stained poor, but on this occasion it was a band of ministers and courtiers he took with him to see Satyavati's father. Ganga D. would always have a penchant for making his most dramatic gestures before a sizeable audience. One day he was even to die in front of a crowd. (23)

The character of Ganga Datta/ Gandhi, with his innumerable fads and his baggage from the hoary antiquity of Hindu India, serves as the major link between the time past and the time present. It is with Gandhi, who reads the Vedas and Tolstoy, the philosophy of Ruskin and the laws of Manu 'with equal involvement' (25), that the mythical story of the novel takes off. Gradually the text gets 'populated by contemporary characters [who are] transported incongruously through time to their oneiric mythological settings' (355). The first half of the novel establishes an almost point-to-point parallel between Bhishma and Gandhi—the Hastinapur patriarch and the undisputed leader of Indian National Congress—from the declaration of his terrible vow of celibacy to his assassination by Shikhandin/Nathuram Godse.

With the expansion of the allegorical scheme, the mythological story encloses other historical characters. Jawaharlal Nehru is represented by Dhritarashtra who 'had the blind man's gift of seeing the world not as it was but as he wanted it to be' (85). Subhas Chandra Bose, the modern Pandu, is presented as a quixotic patriot who lacked pragmatism and judgement. Drawn ironically, though not without sympathy, he is viewed as a leader who could have changed the course of Indian history if he had not been betrayed by both his compatriots and the foreign powers. Mohammed Ali Jinnah is represented by Karna, one of the most interesting, though romanticized, characters in the novel. Tharoor describes in detail the circumstances of his birth and the reasons of his alienation from the Congress Party, which made him join the Muslim League and demand for Pakistan, in order to forge links between Karna and his modern counterpart. The analogy appears to be largely convincing even though modern Karna lacks the beauty, munificence and pathos of his mythical prototype.

In order to fit the actual historical personalities and events into the narrative frame of the epic, Tharoor has made some changes in the cast of characters. Thus, instead of one hundred sons of Dhritarashtra and Gandhari, one finds only Priya Duryodhani who represents all the Kauravas with an altered sex. The Pandavas, on the other hand, are presented as an assorted group and, except Yudhishtir who stands for Morarji Desai, they are conceived as the incarnations of some major institutions of the country like army, press, bureaucracy and foreign service which are meant to husband and protect democracy represented by Draupadi. Regarding these changes, which are necessitated by the narrative design, Tharoor remarks: "the yoking of myth to history restricted some of my fictional options; as the novel progressed, I was obliged to abandon novelistic conventions and develop characters who are merely walking metaphors. Draupadi, thus, became emblematic of Indian democracy, her attempted disrobing a symbol of what was sought to be done to democracy not so long ago."[4] The parentage of the five Pandavas in Tharoor's narrative also does not quite conform to the original. Since Nehru and Indira dominate the political stage in post-independence India, the Pandavas are kept away from the centre of power. They spend most of their time in the countryside with their teacher and political mentor, the bearded socialist Jayaprakash Drona who represents the renowned socialist leader Jayaprakash Narayan. Krishna, the supreme creation of Vyasa in the *Mahabharata,* appears to be a sadly diminished figure in Tharoor's narrative. The epic protagonist is assigned no special role in the novel. He is represented as a small-town M.L.A. and Congress Party secretary who remains aloof from national politics but gives a short spiritual discourse to vacillating Arjun before the election of 1977.

Despite such changes and deviations from the original made to accommodate the principal events and characters of the 20th century India to the plot-outline of the *Mahabharata,* Tharoor has remarkably succeeded in forging smooth and credible connections between the historical and the mythological narratives. The efficacy with which the historic freedom movement and the subsequent conflict among Indian leaders over the issue of sharing power is superimposed on the politico-religious struggle of the epic not only excites interest but also evokes intense reader participation. The responsibility of the reader of *The Great Indian Novel* is to figure out the parallels between the historical and the mythical stories and to grasp their implications in order to make sense of Tharoor's version of the country's past.

NOTES

1. *Seminar*, 384 (August 1991), pp. 30-31.
2. Shashi Tharoor: "Myth, History and Fiction," p. 31.
3. *Littcrit* 16.1-2 (June-December, 1990), 35-44.
4. 'Yoking of Myth to History,' p. 19.

Myth and Mythological Narrative in *The Great Indian Novel*

Myth has often been defined as a complex of stories—some factual and some fictitious—which manifests the deeper meaning of the universe and of human life. It represents man's deepest instinctive life and his primary awareness of the universe. The rediscovery of mythology as a repository of universal emotions and psychological types in the twentieth century prompted creative writers to evince a new interest in the ancient myths. One major reason of this renewed interest in myths was their timelessness and fundamental significance.

Many twentieth century writers consciously used myth as a literary device in their works. In T.S. Eliot's *The Waste Land*, James Joyce's *Ulysses*, and Eugene O'Neill's *Mourning Becomes Electra*, for example, old myths reappear with a new meaning and an immediacy of appeal. O'Neill's play is a fresh rendering of an ancient Greek myth; Joyce's novel reinterprets Homer's *Odyssey* in the context of twentieth century Dublin; and T.S. Eliot uses the Grail legend to depict the spiritual crisis of modern man in the wasteland of war-ravaged Europe. Despite their differences of intentions, scopes and techniques, there is one common factor among these writers. Each of them employs an ancient myth in a contemporary context, thereby attempting to examine the predicament of modern man in a larger perspective of time.

In his famous review of *Ulysses*,[1] T.S. Eliot commended James Joyce for inventing what he called a 'mythical method' in narrating the incidents in the novel: "In using the myth, in manipulating a continuous parallel between contemporaneity and antiquity, Mr. Joyce is pursuing a method which others must pursue after him. . . . It is simply a way of controlling, of ordering, of giving a shape and significance to the immense panorama of futility and anarchy which is contemporary history. . . . Instead of narrative method, we may now use the mythical method." Eliot found an ordering and controlling motive in the mythical elements of *Ulysses* which he himself used in his own poem. He believed that a work of literature could redeem the anarchy and futility of contemporary history by presenting recent events in the critical light of a myth that functions as a coordinate story. Employed in this manner, a myth could redeem the poverty of mere events in a modern narrative. In *Ulysses*, the modern story of Leopold Bloom and the mythical story of Odysseus come from two diametrically opposite levels of discourse. The Homeric story which has acquired, over the centuries, an authority of form and tradition as well as an allusive power, exercises a critical pressure upon the contemporary story. The significance of the novel consists in Joyce's unique method of narration: telling a contemporary story while continuously alluding to the story of Odysseus in Homer's epic. Bloom's adventures in Dublin on June 16, 1904, are not similar to Odysseus's wanderings in the mythic age. But the two narratives resemble each other in form and outline. They also share a pattern of life and this sharing has a value of its own.

An abiding characteristic of the Indian mind has been to discover connections between myth and reality. It has always been conscious of the recurrence of mythic patterns in contemporary events. Characters from the *Ramayana* and the *Mahabharata* are perennial contemporaries for Indians who acknowledge the continuing influence of the two national epics on their private and public lives. The first epigraph to Tharoor's novel—a quotation from C.R. Deshpande's *Transmission of the Mahabharata Tradition*—refers to the lasting influence of Vyasa's epic on India's social and cultural life: "The *Mahabharata* has not only influenced the literature, art, sculpture and painting of India but it has also moulded the very character of the Indian people. Characters from the Great Epic . . . are still household words [which] stand for domestic or public virtues or vices. . . . In India a philosophical or even political controversy can hardly be found that has no reference to the thought of the *Mahabharata*." The second citation, from P. Lal's transcreation of the epic, *The Mahabharata of Vyasa*, suggests its contemporaneity and continuing relevance: "The essential *Mahabharata* is whatever is relevant to us in the second half of the twentieth century. No epic, no work of art, is sacred by itself; if it does not have meaning for me now, it is nothing, it is dead."

The Great Indian Novel is *Mahabharata* re-written in which Shashi Tharoor uses myth elaborately to function as the prototype. The ancient epic of Vyasa provides for Tharoor's novel not only the narrative aesthetics but also a pattern of life as well as a value system to refer to. Tharoor discovers a meaningful correspondence between the new myth of India's freedom struggle and fight for democracy and the epic battle to uphold truth and dharma which took place in the country's fabulous antiquity. The account of recent Indian history in his novel revives the memory of the mythic age and evokes the feeling that contemporary Indian reality can be comprehended in the critical light of the country's mythical past. It suggests that ancient Hastinapur also contained, like present-day India, 'midnight's parents' like Dhritarashtra, Karna, Vidur, and Pandu; villainous advisers like Shakuni; self-seeking and arrogant politicians like Priya Duryodhani whose inordinate greed for power brought about untold misery and suffering to the people. The novel makes a creative use of the mythic material to interpret contemporary history and critically evaluate the role of political personalities of twentieth century India. Tharoor uses the mythic setting as a parallel to the modern age. The remote past and the recent present reflect each other, as in a mirror, and this inter-reflection modifies the reader's usual perception of both the epic and the recent history.

In keeping with the narrative design of the *Mahabharata*, Tharoor's novel begins with the birth of the narrator, Ved Vyas ('The Twice-Born Tale') and ends with the ascent of Yudhishtir to heaven ('The Path to Salvation'). After introducing the narrator, the story moves on to describe the love of Shantanu, king of Hastinapur, for Satyavati (the fisherman's daughter), the appearance of Bhishma, his renunciation of the throne and terrible vow of celibacy to facilitate his father's marriage, and the emergence of Dhritarashtra, Pandu and Vidur. The engineered birth of Pandu's sons, humorously described as 'heir-conditioning' (89), is narrated according to the original account in the epic but Tharoor flavours it with humour and parody. Pandu's 'faithfully infidelious' (86) wives—Kunti and Madri—are presented as ultramodern women who speak English and smoke Turkish cigarettes.

Tharoor makes many such deviations from the original to fit the historical narrative into the narrative frame of the epic. The novel also accommodates a number of incidents from Vyasa's poem—some of them in a slightly modified form—which are not essential for the historical account. For example, the escape of the Pandava brothers from the *Jotugriha* (Lac house), their adventures during the period of exile, Arjun's banishment for a year, his love for and elopement with Subhadra, and his humiliation at the hands of a prostitute named Kameswari. These diverting episodes are introduced to give the novel the amplitude and digressive quality of the epic.

Again, in order to dovetail some important episodes from the epic with the chronological frame of the historical narrative, the novelist shifts them into a dream world. These include the murder of Gandhi, the disrobing of D. Mokrasi during Indira Gandhi's tyrannical rule, and the journey of Yudhishtir to heaven. Tharoor also integrates some key episodes from the *Mahabharata* into the novel in order to project certain important political events of post-independence India allegorically. The defeat of Hidimba by Bhima is presented as a parallel to the liberation of Goa by Indian army from Portuguese occupation; the tearing off of the body of Jarasandha into two halves by the second Pandava mirrors the dismemberment of Pakistan and the creation of Bangladesh. The humiliating defeat of Sahadeva in the wrestling match with Bakasura during the period of exile reflects India's military debacle during the Indo-China war in 1962. *The Great Indian Novel* is, in fact, Tharoor's version of the present-day *Mahabharata*, and as such it is devoid of the original's serious tone. He is neither interested in the epic itself nor reverential towards it. He only uses it as a narrative frame to accommodate a different story.

NOTE

1. T.S. Eliot, "Ulysses, Order, and Myth," *Dial* (November 1923).

Irony and Parody in *The Great Indian Novel*

Thematically Tharoor's novel focuses on the striking analogy between the politico-religious battle of Kurukshetra and the historic freedom struggle against colonial rule. The two are ingeniously blended to create a thematic structure which works simultaneously on two or more levels. The novel is, thus, not an ordinary work of fiction. It becomes a historiographic metafiction in which the novelist uses history as a starting point to revisit the mythical past with parody and irony.

The *Mahabharata*, generally recognized as a multi-dimensional text, is rendered in unequivocal irony and parody in *The Great Indian Novel*. Irony is used in the book not simply as a structural device but also as a mode of perception. This is evident in the parodic nature of the narrator's tone and the attitude he adopts in the text. Tharoor builds up a complex network of meaning on several levels which ultimately results in an extremely sophisticated parody. Parody determines not only the choice of form and the elaboration of subject but also the style and technique of the novel. As an illustration of how parody works in the narrative, one may refer to the opening chapter of Book One ("The Twice-Born Tale") in which Ved Vyas, the narrator, describes Ganapathi who has been sent to him by his old friend Brahm (Brahma) to serve as his scribe: "the next day the chap appeared, the amanuensis. Name of Ganapathi, South Indian, I suppose, with a big nose and shrewd, intelligent eyes. . . . Something about him, elephantine tread, broad forehead and all, impressed me. I agreed" (18).

The irreverent attitude of the narrator towards the divine scribe and the resultant humour and irony all depend on the parodic effect which is deliberately produced by an unlikely combination of tradition and modernity, the past and the present, the sacred and the profane. This stance, maintained throughout the narrative, also creates a complex inter-textuality in the novel. The entire book is based on the idea of inter-textuality of myth and history. *The Great Indian Novel* is a kind of foreground which becomes comprehensible only when the reader is conversant with the background texts, the *Mahabharata* and the history of modern India.

The Historical Narrative in *The Great Indian Novel*

A novel about the textuality of history, *The Great Indian Novel* replaces the unitary myth of India with a comprehensive, though highly subjective, version of the multi-dimensional reality of the country. It reads like a spoof on the official histories of the nation, which are—in Tharoor's opinion—no better than hagiographies, and suggests that the version of an individual recollected from memory can also significantly participate in, and contribute to, the making of national history. The novel takes part in the historiographic contest and presents the pre- and post-independence history of India from the point of view of an individual who is both an insider and a participant.

The remark of Gunter Grass, quoted as the third epigraph in the novel, suggests the overall spirit of Tharoor's historical narrative: "Writers experience another view of history, what's going on, another understanding of 'progress.' . . . Literature must refresh memory." The statement, made in Bombay, stresses the need for fictional reconstruction of history. According to Grass, writers present an alternative version of history which is different from the account of professional historians. The alternative rendering of history through fiction not only challenges the official history of a country provided by hagiographers but also refreshes the people's memory of their past.

The historical narrative in *The Great Indian Novel* begins with the emergence of Mahatma Gandhi as the undisputed leader of Indian struggle for freedom from British rule and ends with the return of Indira Gandhi to power after the premature downfall of the Janata Front government. It covers a period of nearly seventy-five years and all the major political events that took place in pre- and post-independent India: the Champaran Satyagraha, the Jallianwala Bagh massacre, the Salt March, the Round Table Conference, Muslim League's demand for Pakistan, the Quit India Movement, the Partition and Independence of India, her conflicts with Pakistan and China, the Bangladesh War and the Emergency. Gandhiji is represented through Bhishma who is called Ganga Datta to make him appear contemporaneous with our time. Like his mythical archetype, he renounced his claim to power and reared his two young disciples, Dhritarashtra and Pandu (Nehru and Subhas) as his successors.

The novel evinces Gandhi's undisguised preference for Nehru which helped the latter to gain importance in the Congress Party and become the Prime Minister of the country after Independence. It records his role in the resignation of Subhas Chandra Bose from the Congress presidency and his expulsion from the party. Mohammed Ali Jinnah—represented as Karna—was another serious contender for power. He had all the qualities as well as the charisma to lead the Congress Party. But the circumstances of his birth and his monumental ego which would not allow him to accept any subordinate role under Gandhi and Nehru led him to leave the party and espouse the cause of the Muslim League. In post-independence India Nehru was succeeded first by Lal Bahadur Shastri, who was 'a good Prime Minister in his decent and well-meaning way' (317), and then by Indira Gandhi. Indira was chosen as Prime Minister because the old guards of the Congress Party thought that she would remain under their control. But belying all expectations, she soon turned into Frankenstein's monster who threatened the democratic institutions of the country. She tried her best to keep the Pandavas away from power and even to eliminate them.

For the greater part of the narrative, the Pandavas stay away from the corridors of power. They spend their time with their teacher and mentor Jayaprakash Drona (Narayan) in the countryside raising the people's political consciousness, clamouring for land reform and fighting against exploitation and corruption. The marriage of Arjun with D(raupadi) Mokrasi—who has a mixed parentage, being the product of Nehru's illicit liaison with Edwina Mountbatten—allegorically represents the union of Indian democracy with the voice of the people. The Pandavas, however, took an active part in the people's uprising against Indira's misrule, which was led by Jayaprakash Narayan. After her electoral defeat, Yudhishtir (Morarji) became the country's Prime Minister.

Tharoor's alternative version of history critically reassesses the role of leaders like Mahatma Gandhi, Jawaharlal Nehru, Subhas Chandra Bose, Mohammed Ali Jinnah, Indira Gandhi, Jayaprakash Narayan and Morarji Desai. Unlike Rushdie, who preferred Nehru, Tharoor gives greater importance to the role of Gandhiji. The novel presents a compact but rounded portrait of the father of the nation whom contemporary Indians have failed to relate to their lives and hence consigned to the 'mists and myths of historical legend' (47). It recognizes his immense contribution to awaken the people to the evils of British rule.

The narrative depicts the unique manner in which Gandhiji mobilized the Indian masses to fight against colonialism by perfecting the weapons of non-violence, civil disobedience and truth force. It records how he used fasting not only as a means of bringing his principles to life but also as a potent weapon to resist injustice: "In fasting, in directing the strength of his convictions against himself, Gangaji taught us to resist injustice with arms that no one could take away from us. Gangaji's use of the fast made our very weakness a weapon. It captured the imagination of India in a way that no speech, no prayer, no bomb had ever done" (105). Gandhiji widened the mass base of the Congress Party by bringing ordinary men and women into the mainstream of the freedom struggle and thus gave a new orientation to Indian nationalism. Side by side, Tharoor also takes cognizance of his innumerable fads (like taking enema, toilet-cleaning, celibacy, and love for the cows) and his use of Hindu cultural/religious rhetoric which not only galvanized the masses against the British but also alienated nationalist leaders of other communities from the Congress Party. The narrative holds Gandhi unequivocally responsible for Jinnah's disaffection with the Congress: "Karna was not much of a Muslim but he found Gangaji too much of a Hindu. The Mahaguru's traditional attire, his spiritualism, his spouting of the ancient texts, his ashram, his constant harking back to an idealized pre-British past that Karna did not believe in (and was impatient with)—all this made the young man mistrustful of the Great Teacher. . . . A Kaurava Party of prayer-meetings and unselective eclecticism was not a party he would have cared to lead, let alone to remain a member of" (142). It is interesting to note that Tharoor deviates from the widely known account of Gandhiji's death and presents the scene of his murder as a dream-sequence in which Shikhandin (Nathuram Godse)—his assassin—exposes his personal and political weaknesses and declares him to be a failure. The dying words of the father of the nation in Tharoor's narrative are thus not 'Hey Ram' but 'I . . . have . . . failed' (234) which seem to be an admission of Shikhandin's accusation.

Subhas Chandra Bose, Gandhiji's rebellious protégé, is presented ironically but not without sympathy. The novel commends his courageous efforts in the cause of freedom but it shows how he perished because of his lack of judgement and his impractical dreams. The modern prototype of mythical Pandu is viewed as a leader who could have changed the course of Indian history had he not been betrayed at home and abroad by his own party and by foreign powers. Mohammed Ali Jinnah, the exponent of the Two-Nation theory, is exalted and romanticized by Tharoor in the guise of Karna 'whose golden skin glowed like a sun and on whose forehead shone the bright little half moon that became his party's symbol' (133). The mystery surrounding his birth made him an archetypal outsider like Kunti's pre-marital offspring. The novel narrates in detail the reasons of his alienation from the Congress Party which made him join the Muslim League and demand a separate Muslim homeland.

The portrait of Nehru presented in the novel is not at all a flattering one. It seems to balance the (indiscriminately laudatory) account of Nehru's role in the country's politics given by official hagiographers of the Congress Party and government. The basic idea of his role is derived from that of blind Dhritarashtra: 'He had the blind man's gift of seeing the world not as it was, but as he wanted it to be' (85). This metaphorical blindness, together with his monumental ego and vaulting ambition, made him an appropriate prototype of Dhritarashtra. The narrative clearly suggests that he gained importance in the party hierarchy and defeated Subhas in the race for power because of Gandhiji's blessings. It does not conceal his unholy liaison with Edwina Mountbatten who was used by her wily husband as a 'secret weapon' to charm Indian leaders. The novel accuses him of ignoring the appeal of Gandhiji and agreeing to the hasty and heedless deal of partition at the behest of Mountbatten and his wife. It chronicles how, as the country's first Prime Minister, he 'bungled' the Kashmir issue and evinced his lack of foresight by unilaterally taking it to the United Nations. Nehru's major domestic and foreign policies are severely criticized as being ill-conceived and utopian. Tharoor traces the reasons of his mistakes to his shortsightedness: 'Dhritarashtra was guilty only of the insincerity of the blind' (295). The only credit that he gives to India's first Prime Minister is that he was, despite his limitations and drawbacks, a true democrat.

Like Nehru, his daughter Indira Gandhi, too, is presented in an unfavourable light. Though the narrative delineates her lonely and neglected childhood spent by the bedside of her perennially sick mother, she is cast in the role of female Duryodhan—Priya Duryodhani: an ironic combination of Indira Priyadarshini and Duryodhan. It is because of her arrogance, selfishness, scheming nature, intolerance and undemocratic instinct to eliminate her political rivals, she is conceived of as a modern counterpart of Dhritarashtra's eldest child. The narrative shows how, after being elected as the Prime Minister following Lal Bahadur Shastri's death, she tried to entrench herself by implementing, with the help of the left and progressive parties in the Parliament which were duped by her socialist rhetoric and lip-service to the poor and the downtrodden, a series of populist measures like bank nationalization that proved ultimately detrimental to the country's economics. She systematically undermined all the democratic institutions in the country and promoted the culture of empty slogans. The novel depicts how she 'smashed all the pillars and foundations' of 'the world's oldest anti-colonial political organization' (351), and allowed herself to be 'surrounded by the recumbent forms of . . . supplicants prostrating themselves amidst the rubble' (351). The political totalitarianism under Indira's rule is subjected to a cynical scrutiny in the narrative: "Her speech-writers peppered her rhetoric with dutiful obeisance to the wretched of the Indian earth, she proclaimed her democratic pedigree and socialist convictions from every lectern and platform—and she acquired more and more power in their name. . . . She squeezed the newsprint supplies of the press because they were 'out of touch' with the masses . . . she fettered the judiciary by demanding they be 'committed' to the people . . . she emasculated her party by appointing its state leaders rather than allowing them to be elected (for she alone could judge who best would serve the people)" (357).

The proclamation of the Emergency by Indira after the historic verdict of the Allahabad High Court is evaluated somewhat differently by Tharoor. While writers like Rushdie have viewed Emergency as the single most traumatic event in post-independence Indian politics and the starting point of the degradation of the country's secular polity, Tharoor considers it as the culmination of the country's degenerating political culture since Independence. He criticizes Indira's decision to impose the Siege on the people as 'primarily cynical and self-serving' but also blames opposition leaders like Jayaprakash Narayan whose unremitting attack compelled the beleaguered Prime Minister to take this extreme step. The narrator, Ved Vyas, thus, remarks: "I still believed that the political chaos in the country, fuelled by Drona's idealistic but confused Uprising which a variety of political opportunists had joined and exploited, could have led the country nowhere but to anarchy" (369).

The protagonist of 1977s silent revolution which defeated totalitarian tendencies in Indian politics and restored freedom and democracy, is called a 'saintly anarchist' (269) in Tharoor's account. In his obituary after Jayaprakash's death, Ved Vyas pays a glowing tribute to this 'secular saint' for his unwavering 'commitment to truth and justice' and his steadfast 'loyalty to the ideals of a democratic and egalitarian India,' but reproves him for allowing 'the revolution he had wrought fall into the hands of lesser men who were unworthy of his ideals' (409). His historical narrative of twentieth century India ends as 'a story of betrayed expectations' (411). He finds an all-pervasive degradation of political values and standards and visualizes a bleak future for the country.

The Great Indian Novel as a Postcolonial Text

A paradigmatic postcolonial text, *The Great Indian Novel* gives expression to the colonized experience and undermines the colonialst discourse. It seeks to rewrite the history of India's colonial encounter from a postcolonial point of view.

After the dismantling of Empire, it was widely felt that the history of the colonized people, severely damaged by the colonial rule, needed repair. The reclamation of history, which included the retrieval of oral memory, was believed to be an important process through which the impaired self of a nation could be remade. Adaptation of indigenous myth was regarded as another important mode of retrieval of the past. Using myths drawn from native tradition, postcolonial writers sought to integrate the cultural life of the past with their post-independence reality. They turned to their own cultural traditions both as the source of a new national identity and as a mythic resource with which they structured their works.

The urge to rewrite the past became particularly acute in those countries where the European colonizers represented the pre-conquest past as a blank or a backward space devoid of civilization and culture. Challenging the governing topos of colonialist representation that India was an underdeveloped country, a backward space, the octogenarian narrator of *The Great Indian Novel*, thus, asserts: "India is not an underdeveloped country but a highly developed one in an advanced state of decay" (17). As a postcolonial text, Tharoor's novel not only rewrites the country's pre-independence history but also critically scrutinizes the colonial relationship and resists colonialist perspectives. It challenges the ideologically determined patterns of historical relationship.

In Ved Vyas's alternative account, the native people of India do not play only side-roles in British history, as in the novels of Rudyard Kipling, E.M. Forster, M.M. Kaye, and Paul Scott; they rather make history. In those sections of the novel which describe the colonial past, Tharoor debunks the literary myths which sustained the Empire and shatters the idols of imperial history.

The book seeks to emancipate the formerly colonized people from the reverential awe in which they held the colonizers. The impressive figure of Mountbatten (represented as Viscount Drewpad) is significantly reduced to a shallow, vainglorious and insensitive individual who 'wore his lack of learning lightly' (211), and General Reginald Dyer (fictionalized as Rudyard Kipling) is remembered as an inhuman tyrant. Edwina Mountbatten (Georgina Drewpad) is depicted as an 'amatory adventuress of libellous renown' (229) who was used by her husband as a 'secret-weapon' (215) to charm and win over Indian leaders. Tharoor ruthlessly attacks British colonialism through his caricature/parody of imperialist rulers and attempts to link many of the ills which plague independent India to the mischief done by the British during their rule. The narrative takes cognizance of the pernicious effects of indoctrination of Indian school children by 'the bastard educational institutions the British sired on us' (47), and the disastrous consequences of the imperial policy of 'divide and rule' for the Indian subcontinent (133-36). Ved Vyas's oral narrative attempts to supplant the recorded British history of colonized India with a counter discourse that subverts and undermines the colonizers' view of the country. He uses, like Rushdie, the 'novel of memory' as a political weapon to disprove the imperialists' version of truth and resist the forgetfulness which is induced by their distortion, even alteration, of historical facts.

Tharoor's narrative contains a trenchant critique of colonial attitudes and policies. The historical account of the novel begins around the end of the nineteenth century when colonialism had consolidated into a tyrannical system. The disparaging attitude of the colonizers to native languages and culture was illustrated by Sir Richard, the British Resident in Hastinapur, who said, echoing Macaulay, to his aide Ronald Heaslop: "These native languages don't really have much to them, you know. And it's not as if you have to write poetry in them. A few crucial words, sufficient English for ballast, and you're sailing smoothly." (37).

The novel records how the colonial policy led to the starvation of Indian peasants: "There was starvation in Motihari, not just because the land did not produce enough for its tillers to eat, but because it could not, under the colonialists' laws, be entirely devoted to keeping them alive. Three tenths of every man's land had to be consecrated to indigo" (51). While commenting on the Jallianwala Bagh massacre, the narrator lays bare the inhumanity of the colonial ethics and the hollowness of the claim that the imperialists were carrying on a 'civilizing mission' in India made by British writers and historians who provided the theoretical underpinning for colonialism: "Or perhaps he just acted in the way dictated by the simple logic of colonialism, under which the rules of humanity applied only to the rulers, for the rulers were people and the people were objects. Objects to be controlled, disciplined, kept in their place and taught lessons like so many animals: yes, the civilizing mission upon which Rudyard and his tribe were embarked made savages of all of us, and all of them." (80)

The Jallianwala Bagh massacre, called the Bibigarh Gardens massacre in the novel to parody the infamous Bibigarh rape in Paul Scott's Raj fiction *The Day of the Scorpion*, is narrated with an irony and objectivity that only matches the spirit of its description in Rushdie's *Midnight's Children*: "The soldiers fired just 1600 bullets that day, Ganapathi. It was so mechanical, so precise; they used up only the rounds they were allocated, nothing was thrown away, no additional supplies sent for. Just 1600 bullets into the unarmed throng, and when they had finished, oh, perhaps ten minutes later, 379 people lay dead, Ganapathi, and 1,137 lay injured, many grotesquely maimed. When Rudyard was given the figures later he expressed satisfaction with his men. 'Only 84 bullets wasted,' he said. 'Not bad'" (81).

The brutality of the imperialists and their complete lack of human feelings led the narrator to arrive at the conclusion that 'the Raj was not just evil but Satanic' (83). He ruthlessly exposes the loot of India's fabulous wealth by the British merchants: 'the merchants and adventurers and traders of the East India Company . . . came to an India that was fabulously rich and prosperous, they came in search of wealth and profit, and they took what they could take, leaving Indians to wallow in their leavings' (95). The exploitative aspect of the colonial rule and its harmful effect on the country's economy have also been stressed: "The British killed the Indian artisan, they created the Indian 'landless labourer,' they exported our full-employment and they invented our poverty" (95). The narrative not only makes a critical assessment of British colonial administrators in India ('The truth is that the average British colonial administrator was a pompous mediocrity whose nose was so often in the air that he tripped over his own feet' [116]), but also denounces their 'divide and rule' policy ('The strategy was amoral, the tactics immoral' [135]) which resulted in India's partition, and the haphazard division of the country on the basis of religion which led to unprecedented violence and mass exodus.

The period of British rule is, thus, for Tharoor, a fitting target for hilarious lampoons and impassioned frontal attacks. The excesses of the British Raj are brilliantly mocked at. Side by side, the novel also depicts the country's struggle against colonial rule under the dynamic leadership of Mahatma Gandhi which heralded 'the dawn of a new epoch': "Students left their classes in the city colleges to flock to Gangaji's side; small-town lawyers abandoned the security of their regular fees at the assizes to volunteer for the cause; journalists left the empty debating halls of the nominated council chambers to discover the real heart of the new politics. A nation was rising, with a small, balding, semi-clad saint at its head" (51).

Many of the chapters in Tharoor's novel are given titles which parody well-known literary works on India by British authors like Paul Scott, Rudyard Kipling, M.M. Kaye and E.M. Forster. There are chapters with titles like 'The Duel with the Crown,' 'A Raj Quartet,' 'The Powers of Silence,' 'Passages through India,' 'The Man Who Could not be King,' 'The Far Power-Villain' (which is reminiscent of Kaye's *The Far Pavillions*) and 'The Bungle Book' (that reminds one of Kipling's *Jungle Book*). Some of these authors and characters of their novels reincarnate as colonial figures in Tharoor's narrative. Rony Heaslop of Forster's *A Passage to India*, for example, reappears in *The Great Indian Novel* as a typical representative of the colonial rule who is contemptuous of the natives and their culture. Maurice Forster, who is just down from Cambridge and 'seems to prefer young boys,' recalls E.M. Forster. Rudyard Kipling is represented as Colonel Rudyard, an insensitive and tyrannical army officer who orders his soldiers to open fire on an unarmed crowd in Bibigarh Gardens. The parody of the colonialist literature written by and for the British about India, which embodied the imperialists' point of view and was informed by theories regarding the superiority of European culture and the rightness of Empire, is a subtle but powerful reversal, by Shashi Tharoor, of the traditional tide of cultural colonialism.

The Great Indian Novel as a Postmodernist Work

It is generally believed that Indian English novel made a quantum leap from modernism to postmodernism with the appearance of the Rushdie generation in 1980s. It was Rushdie who blazed the trail. His novels illustrate the aesthetic style of postmodernism. *Midnight's Children* (1981), which marked the turning point, is regarded as a paradigmatic postmodern text which celebrates fragmentation, multiplicity and self-reflexivity, and insists on the provisional nature of all truths. This book, like *The Satanic Verses* (1989), takes liberty with the hallowed tradition and the conventions of history and fiction writing. In both the novels Rushdie rejects totalizing world-views, challenges sacred absolutes, and acknowledges the fact that reality is nothing but an imperfect construct of the human mind. *The Great Indian Novel* (1989) is, like Rushdie's pioneering works, a postmodernist text which re-writes the ancient Indian epic, the *Mahabharata*, for an irreverent, humorous and highly entertaining spoof of recent Indian history. It fulfils all the major features of postmodernism, both in theory and in practical applications.

II

Before going to the discussion of how Shashi Tharoor has introduced the postmodernist insight into his novel, it may be worthwhile to know the basic tenets of the phenomenon known as postmodernism. The postmodernist writers like Thomas Pynchon, John Barth, Carlos Fuentes, Donald Barthelme, and their theoretical counterparts like Jacques Derrida, Michel Foucault, Roland Barthes, Jacques Lacan, J.F. Lyotard et. al. acknowledge that the Western civilization has arrived at a point beyond consensus, at a fragmented time in which doubt, anxiety and a kind of rudderlessness dominate life. They recognize the fundamental instability of the world where meaning is a hopeless delusion and knowledge is contingent.

Derrida, for example, argues that no meaning exists beyond language and that discourse is severed from the world. The world of meaning fragments, making it difficult to speak of meaning in the conventional sense. In his seminal work, *Of Grammatology*, Derrida defines the science of writing ('grammatology') as the science of 'the arbitrariness of sign' (1974: 51).[1] Writing is seen by him as the endless displacement of meaning which governs language and at the same time places it beyond the reach of a stable knowledge. There is no transcendental signified which is meaningful in itself and which escapes the ceaseless interplay of linguistic deferral and difference. Therefore, the search for meaning, truth and presence is futile. The belief that there is, or ever was, a reality is a delusion or a myth on which people build their metaphysical notions of origin and truth. In Derrida's contingent world of textuality there is an indeterminacy which makes both consistency and certainty impossible. The text, in his view, should be regarded as a slippery, deceptive narrative which never achieves any stability. This stress on the indeterminacy of language undermines the logo-centric stance of modernism. With the disappearance of the grounds for meaning, the search for any distinction between the real and the unreal, the true and the untrue becomes a bootless exercise. In what is now regarded as one of the most significant documents of poststructuralist critical theory, 'Structure, Sign, and Play in the Discourse of the Human Sciences,'[2]

Derrida introduces the concept of 'decentering,' of the 'structurality of structure' by which he means that outside discourse there is no centre or fixed point from which one can establish metaphysical boundaries for linguistic signifiers. The desire for a centre is dismissed by Derrida as part of the old metaphysics, 'the metaphysics of presence.' The postmodernist writers accept uncertainty as the only constant, change as the only certain thing. Wholeness and certitude are no longer possible; fragmentation, uncertainty, ambiguity and doubt are accepted as part of life. This decentering, negation of certitude and replacement of fixity by multiplicity are the essentials of postmodernist sensibility.

Whereas the Derridan strategy of deconstruction raises serious questions about texts and deprives them of any stability, Ronald Barthes (in his essay 'From Work to Text,' 1971) regards the text as a methodological field, as something that can be experienced as an activity, or even a production. He insists on the infinite multiplicity of a given text. A text is, according to Barthes, always heterogeneous or plural. While Derrida evinces the unattainability of the whole, Michel Foucault questions the very possibility of acquiring knowledge and of giving an account of the world. The boundaries between knowledge and world or text and interpretation thus cease to exit. A text is always rewritten and reworked by its consumers. Its ultimate sense is derived not on the printed page but, as Stanley Fish shows, in the reader's mind. The Author is removed from the text because, as Roland Barthes argues in 'The Death of the Author,'[3] 'to give a text an Author is to impose a limit on that text, to furnish it with a final signified, to close the writing.'

The rejection of the notion of a text as an organic whole, of meaning and representation, of 'myths of origin' and 'metaphysics of presence,' of any ideology that claims to have a complete or totalized explanation of the world ('incredulity towards metanarratives,' in Lyotard's famous formulation), and the acceptance of the fragmentation of truth, of the fact that 'all that is solid has melted into air, that reality and morality are not givens but imperfect human constructs'[4] are what Lyotard called, in 1979, '*La Condition Postr oderne.*' But while the modernist writers like Eliot, Pound and Joyce cultivated an aesthetic of despair in the face of fractured experience and loss of certitude, the postmodernists propel the sense of loss in a celebratory direction. They exude a sense of *jouissance*, relaxing "in a playground of irony and irreverent pastiche, where pluralism and difference contrast with the older 'terrorism' of totalizing discourses."[5]

Postmodernism is essentially subversive; it disregards and disrupts almost everything in the tradition. It challenges the validity of the received notions of language, the text, the Author, the power of authority and the role of history. By giving a farewell to meaning and "refusing to assign a 'secret' or ultimate meaning to the text (and to the world as text),"[6] and by denying the existence of an absolute, transcendental value, the postmodernists have made a radical swing from theoretical certainty to uncertainty. They have called in question every aspect of realism–like history, fixedness, identifiable representation–which was once taken for granted. They present a universe which is devoid of the assurance of Truth or of the possibility of a final knowledge. Living in an age cut adrift from the traditional value system, the postmodernists prefer doubt and suspicion to certitude and conviction and they view their task as defamiliarization, decentering and deconstruction.

III

In *The Great Indian Novel*, Tharoor takes his readers down through the country's 'tryst with destiny,' with the leading figures from contemporary history cast in the mould of great epic characters. Gandhiji, for example, is cast in the role of Bhishma, the celibate Kaurava patriarch who is obsessed with Truth, non-violence, untouchability and toilet-cleaning. He is referred to in the novel as Gangaji (Ganga Dutta) and described by the British Viceroy, Sir Richard, as 'Public Enema Number One' (113). Dhritarashtra is the blind son of Vichitravirya and a favourite disciple of Gangaji. He has a weakness for Fabian socialism and is a fatal charmer of the ladies of Bloomsbury. He 'found education in India a harrowing experience' (41) and was sent to England where he acquired 'traces of the right accent along with streaks of the wrong ideas.' (110) Later he became the country's first Prime Minister. Pandu, his pale brother, was expelled from one of the best colleges of the country for striking a British teacher who had called Indians dogs. Fed up of the non-violent ways of his mentor, Gangaji, he stormed off to Germany and then to Japan to seek fascist help for the country's liberation: '"Away with Tolstoy, Ruskin, Buddha./Their ideas just make little men littler./ No more "truth-force," only *yuddha—*/ It's time to learn from that chap Hitler."' (177)

Mohammed Ali Karna, the fruit of the error of Kunti's adolescence and adopted son of a rich man's driver, is the lawyer disciple of Gangaji. He has a sun-like glow on his face, which distinguishes him from others, and he likes cocktail sausages. He becomes the founder of the Muslim state Karnistan, a country which is carved out of India and which Priya Duryodhani will help split to form Gelabi Desh. The teacher of the five Pandava brothers, who had an engineered birth ('heir-conditioning,' [89]), is a bearded socialist named Jayaprakash Drona.

The narrative begins with Gangaji's emergence as a national leader and his election as the President of the Kaurava Party which led the country to freedom, and which split after Independence, one side going to Priya Duryodhani, Dhritarashtra's only child with the famous arched brow who, as Prime Minister, imposed a 'siege' on the country. It ends with the death of Duryodhani, her murder by her own security guards. The historical narrative follows the line of the *Mahabharata*, providing insight into both current politics and the epic. The old narrator, Ved Vyas, tells in his story—which is dictated to his amanuensis, the elephant-headed Ganapathi—'of past, present and future, of existence and passing, of efflorescence and decay, of death and rebirth; of what is, of what was, of what should have been' (18). But in this 'definitive memoir of [his] life and times' which is, he claims, 'nothing less than *The Great Indian Novel*' (18), history is transformed into myth and the epic characters become figures of contemporary history. The dividing lines between fact and fiction, myth and history become blurred.

The novel inhabits a world of multiple realities and of multiple interpretations of reality. The reader is amazed to find that his knowledge of Indian history and myths is no authentic guide to reality. There is such an indeterminacy in the text that neither certainty not stability is possible. The text becomes an elusive, unknowable narrative which never provides any certitude or stable knowledge. Well-known facts of history and ancient legends are presented in a new, unfamiliar way. Many of the characters, incidents and issues in this novel are based on people and events described in the great epic. But Tharoor has taken too many liberties with them. In *Afterword*, he writes, "While some scenes in *The Great Indian Novel* are recastings of situations described in translations of the *Mahabharata*, I have taken far too many liberties with the epic." Again, the lives, deeds and even famous utterances of historical figures like Gandhi, Nehru, Subhas Chandra Bose, Jinnah, Maulana Abul Kalam Azad and Mountbatten are changed to depict familiar matters in an unfamiliar way. Many of these respected leaders go down like nine pins in the novel just as the *dramatis personae* of the epic receive a severe bruising.

Similarly, historical events of India's struggle for freedom and her subsequent experiment with democracy are re-organized to suit the novelist's fiction, much in the same way as Rushdie did in *Midnight's Children*. The result is defamiliarisation, demystification, and negation of history. There is no clue to reality; nothing can be taken for granted in the uncertain fictional world of Tharoor. Underlining ambiguity and negating history, the text subverts closure and suggests alternatives. The narrator says: "for every tale I have told . . . every perception I have conveyed, there are a hundred equally valid alternatives I have omitted and of which you are unaware. . . . This is my story of the India I know, with its biases, selections, omissions, distortions, all mine. But you can not derive your cosmogony from a single birth, Ganapathi. Every Indian must for ever carry with him, in his head and heart, his own history of India" (373). It becomes what Roland Barthes would call a 'creative text' which resists finality and remains open to doubt and uncertainty.

There is, Shashi Tharoor seems to suggest, more than one Truth, more than one way of looking at the history and myths which have shaped Indian people and their culture. At one point the narrator says, almost echoing Saleem Sinai in *Midnight's Children*, that the novel is his version of reality: "It is my truth, Ganpathi, just as the crusade to drive out the British reflected Gangaji's truth, and the fight to be rid of both the British and the Hindu was Karna's truth. Which philosopher would dare to establish a hierarchy among such verities?" (164) He asks, "Is it permissible to modify truth with a possessive pronoun?" (164) There is no clear answer in the text but the author seems to suggest that it is permissible.

By accepting the multiplicity of truths and acknowledging the multiple versions of reality as equally valid, Tharoor catches up with the western postmodernist writers who have asserted the end of the Truth. Like them he insists on the provisional nature of all truths: 'All knowledge is transient, linked to the world around it and subject to change as the world changes' (163). Therefore, he does not claim any finality for his story: "What happened in the end? . . . 'the end' was an idea that . . . meant nothing to me. I did not begin the story in order to end it; the essence of the tale lay in the telling. 'What happened next?' I could answer, but 'what happened in the end?' I could not even understand." (162) There is, he believes, no end to the story of life, there are only pauses: 'The end is the arbitrary invention of the teller, but there can be no finality about his choice.' (163) Thus Truth and history are given a terrible jolt in the novel and traditional assumptions like finality, fixity, certitude and identifiable representation are rejected.

Like other postmodernist writers, Tharoor finds no certitude in any particular ideology or dogma, in any particular view of history and myth. Since history, 'indeed the world, the universe, all human life, and so, too, every institution under which we live—is in a constant state of evolution' (245), since all knowledge is transient and suffers from the crippling defect of ephemerality, one must accept doubt and diversity. Thus his Yudhishtir declaims at the end of the novel: 'there are no classical verities valid for all time.' And he proclaims: "No more certitudes. . . . Accept doubt and diversity. Let each man live by his own code of conduct, so long as he has one. Derive your standards from the world around you and not from a heritage whose relevance must be constantly tested. Reject equally the sterility of ideologies and the passionate prescriptions of those who think themselves infallible. . . . Admit that there is more than one Truth, more than one Right, more than one dharma." (418)

By upsetting all certitudes, *The Great Indian Novel* illustrates in fictional terms what the deconstructionist critics describe as 'difference.' It accepts the impossibility or unattainability of a centre and celebrates diversity, fragmentation of truth, anxiety and doubt. At the end, the narrator, Ved Vyas, wakes up from his dream in today's India, a 'land of computers and corruptions, of myths and politicians and box-wallahs with moulded plastic briefcases. To an India beset with uncertainties, muddling chaotically through to the twenty-first century.' (418) And he wants to dream again; he wants to retell his story. Because his last dream, which comprises the narrative, leaves him with a serious problem: 'If it means . . . anything at all, it means that I have told my story so far from a completely mistaken perspective' (418). There is a circularity about the narrative; it ends where it began, the last line of the book being the same as its opening line.

Stylistically, too, Tharoor finds the traditional rules of fiction writing inadequate for his novel. His is a self-reflexive work whose matter or substance consists in defining its own creation. It attempts to undermine itself as a reality by constantly emphasizing its fictional basis. Tharoor introduces a narrator who consciously interacts with the reader and the text as one often finds in the eighteenth century fiction: "Right, Ganapathi? So, we've got the genealogies out of the way, my progeny are littering the palace at Hastinapur, and good old Ganga Dutta is still safely ensconced as regent. No, on second thoughts, you'd better cut out that adverb. 'Safely' wouldn't be entirely accurate. A new British Resident, successor of the bewhiskered automobilist, is in place and is far from sure he likes what is going on" (35). In this way, the text becomes a metafiction as it focuses on the very process in which it comes into being. And since this high degree of self-consciousness is extended to the area of history writing, it also becomes historiographic metafiction.

The novel also illustrates the authorial involvement with the reader and the text as opposed to the practice of the modernist writers who laid emphasis on objectivity. There is an indeterminacy in his form of expression. He makes no distinction between fact and fiction, history and legend, prose and poetry. He occasionally breaks into poetry and light verse and thus affirms the ineffectiveness of standard English prose for his story. Tharoor uses the broader base of fiction as a stepping stone to unite the two different genres of poetry and fiction. He fictionalizes the traditional poetic epic and synthesizes it with politics. By doing so, he contributes to the well-known 'blurring of the genre' of postmodernism. *The Great Indian Novel* is a highly subversive work; it debunks both the ancient epic and the modern myths of Indian freedom struggle. It repudiates the purity of Indian democracy and its established narrative. There is a character in the novel called Draupadi Mokrasi—often referred to as D. Mokrasi—born on January 26, 1950, as a result of the illicit, clandestine union between Dhritarashtra and Georgina Drewpad, wife of Viscount Drewpad who oversees the transfer of power and the partition of India.

Like Rushdie, Tharoor takes too much liberty with the old and venerable tradition. He also assumes a parodic stance to his mythic material and seems to suggest that all narratives—whether epic or historical—are subject to re-interpretation and re-writing. Deconstructions of the canonical text as well as the socio-political, religious and cultural myths of the country, and dismantling of the underlying assumptions are Shashi Tharoor's lasting contribution to Indian writing in English.

It must, however, be mentioned at the end that the postmodernist sensibility manifest in *The Great Indian Novel* bears an affinity with the Indian view of reality. At one point in his narrative, Ved Vyas says, "How easily we Indians see the several sides to every question! That is what makes us such good bureaucrats, and such poor totalitarians. They say the new international organizations set up by the wonderfully optimistic (if oxymoronic) United Nations are full of highly successful Indian officials with quick, subtle minds . . . for ever able to understand every global crisis from the point of view of each and every one of the contending parties. That is why they do so well . . . in any situation that calls for an instinctive awareness of the subjectivity of truth, the relativity of judgement and the impossibility of action" (373). Notions like multiplicity, indeterminacy, circularity, absence of finality and the impossibility of getting at the Truth are articulated, for example, in the epistemological view of Jainism which appeared as a protest movement against the supreme authority of the *Vedas* that firmly believed in the existence of the transcendental Supreme Reality. Jainism views reality as pluralistic and relative and it looks upon any quest for the absolute as futile.

The novel's insight may, thus, be said to be an offshoot of India's pluralistic culture. It grows out of, and speaks for, an India that acknowledges and welcomes multiplicity and honours all interpretations of reality, of the world and the text as potentially valid. The book gains an added significance in this troubled time of religious intolerance or dogmatism which wants to proclaim the supremacy of one religion, one God, and one interpretation of reality.

NOTES

4. Jacques Derrida, *Of Grammatology* (1974, French), Glas. Paris: Galilee. Cited in Christopher Norris' *Deconstruction: Theory and Practice* (London, Methuen, 1982).

1. Jacques Derrida, 'Structure, Sign, and Play in the Discourse of the Human Sciences,' *The Structuralist Controversy: The Languages of Criticism and the Sciences of Man*, ed. Richard Macksey and Eugenio Donato (Baltimore, 1972), pp. 247-65.
2. Ronald Barthes, 'The Death of the Author,' (1977), *Twentieth-Century Literary Theory: A Reader*, ed. K.M. Newton (London:

Macmillan, 1988), p. 157.

3. Salman Rushdie, 'Is Nothing Sacred?,' *Imaginary Homelands* (London, Granta Books, 1991), p. 422.
4. David Lyon, *Postmodernity* (New Delhi: Viva Books, 2002), p. 97.
5. Ronald Barthes, 'The Death of the Author.'

The Great Indian Novel: A Detailed Analysis of the Text

The Great Indian Novel is a large, sprawling novel with a loose, episodic structure. It is modelled on the ancient epic of Vyasa, the *Mahabharata*, in terms of both structure and issues. The novel is divided into eighteen books which are skilfully planned as parallels to the cantos of Vyasa's epic. The books are given titles which parody well-known literary works on India by British and Indian authors and display the intertextuality of the novel. There are chapters entitled 'The Duel with the Crown,' 'A Raj Quartet' and 'The Powers of Silence' which recall the Raj fiction of Paul Scott. The chapter named 'Passages through India' is a fitting reply to E.M. Forster's famous novel *A Passage to India*. While 'The Bungle Book,' which narrates the tyrannical rule of Indira Gandhi, reminds one of Rudyard Kipling's *The Jungle Book*, 'The Far Power Villain' is reminiscent of M.M. Kaye's *The Far Pavillicns*. The author's debt to Salman Rushdie is tacitly acknowledged in entitling a chapter 'Midnight's Parents.'

The novel synchronizes the epic narrative of the *Mahabharata* and the twentieth century political history of India. It covers the period of Indian history from the advent of Mahatma Gandhi as the undisputed leader of the freedom struggle against the British Raj to the Emergency rule of Indira Gandhi, highlighting en route some landmark events like the Champaran satyagraha, the Jallianwala Bagh massacre, the Salt March, the Quit India movement, the Partition of India and Independence, the country's war with Pakistan and China, the birth of Bangladesh and the dismemberment of the Land of the Pure, the horror of the Emergency and its aftermath. The shape and sequential drift of the novel is dictated by the epic narrative of the *Mahabharata* which provides Tharoor with an appropriate allegorical framework to project the modern Indian situation. The epic, which has a solid historical core and embraces virtually all the aspects of human experience, becomes a suitable model for Tharoor's fictional reconstruction of national history. *The Great Indian Novel* centres on themes and concerns which one also finds at the core of the epic narrative: power, politics, schisms, conspiracy, personality clashes leading to fratricidal war, institutional structures, and individual as well as collective dharma.

Through a creative use of the mythic setting, Tharoor builds up an order where the ancient and the modern, the past and the present are inextricably entwined. Instead of using two separate time-frames—one for the epic age and the other for the modern—he fuses them into one, presenting events, episodes and characters from the *Mahabharata* as contemporaneous with the present. One thus finds a simultaneous description of the ancient and the modern reality, each mirroring the other and modifying the reader's perception of both. Tharoor uses the allegorical mode in which the story of the *Mahabharata* becomes a structuring device to create an individual and highly subjective/ subversive version of India's past and offers an incisive commentary on the political events and personalities of twentieth century India.

In conformity with the narrative design of the *Mahabharata*, Tharoor begins his account with the birth of the narrator, Ved Vyas ('The Twice-Born Tale') and ends with the Pandavas' journey to heaven ('The Path to Salvation'). In between, he narrates, following the epic pattern, the story of India's glorious anti-colonial struggle and her disappointing postcolonial destiny.

Book I: *The Twice-Born Tale*

The opening chapter closely follows the epic and establishes the genealogy of the Kaurava clan. It begins with a description of the birth of the narrator Ved Vyas, out of wedlock, from the union of Parasar, a wandering Brahmin sage, and Satyavati, a fisherman's daughter. It then moves on to narrate the appearance of

Ganga Datta (the son of king Shantanu and his consort, Ganga) who was made heir-apparent of Hastinapur's throne; the love of Shantanu and Satyavati; Ganga Datta's renunciation of his claim to the throne in order to facilitate the marriage of his father with the fisherman's daughter and his terrible vow of celibacy which made him widely known as Bhishma.

After Shantanu's death, his young son Vichitravirya became Hastinapur's king, with bachelor Gangaji as his regent. After his renunciation of power and vow of celibacy, Ganga Datta had begun to immerse himself in the great works of the past and the present, reading the Vedas and Tolstoy, the *Gita* and the Bible, the laws of Manu and the philosophy of Ruskin with equal zest. His manner became 'other-worldly' (26) and he was increasingly absorbed with religious philosophy, sexual forbearance and personal fads like taking enema, fasts, toilet cleaning and love for the cow. Highlighting this aspect of Ganga/Gandhi's personality in which he would often lapse into timelessness, the narrator remarks, "he would often startle his audiences with pronouncements which led them to wonder in which century he was living at any given moment" (26). But as regent, he dutifully attended to the affairs of the state. When the time came for his half-brother's marriage, Ganga/ Bhishma forcefully abducted the three beautiful daughters of the king of Kashi, a northern princedom, from their *swayamvara* ceremony and brought them to Hastinapur. As the eldest of the three sisters—Amba—had already given her heart to king Salva of Saubal, Gangaji sent her back to her lover and arranged the marriage of the other two—Ambika and Ambalika—with his ward. Amba met with a terrible fate. Rejected by both Salva and Vichitravirya, she came back to Ganga Datta, whom she held responsible for her plight, and requested him to save her honour. But Bhishma refused to break his vow. Doomed to a life of disgrace and spinsterhood, the distraught princess 'forgot all but her searing hatred for her well-intentioned abductor' (29) and took an unbreakable vow to take revenge on him.

Meanwhile his sexual excess had driven debauched Vichitravirya into a 'fatally priapic state' and the king died of 'terminal concupiscence' (30) without leaving any heir. The political narrative takes off from this critical moment in the history of Hastinapur, with the threat of annexation by the British dangling over the princely state like the sword of Damocles after the untimely death of Vichitravirya. The state of Hastinapur without an heir was comparable to the state of Indian National Congress which was divided into the moderates and the extremists, none of whom were recognized by the British as the true representative of the native people. But Ganga Datta firmly took charge of the affairs of Hastinapur and foiled the British attempt to take over the state.

Satyavati, whose desire to see her own child on the throne had deprived Ganga of marital bliss, now approached him anxiously. She requested her stepson to impregnate his widowed sisters-in-law for the sake of dynasty. But Ganga Datta remained true to his principle and advised his stepmother to approach her first son Ved Vyas/ Dvaipayan. The latter, however, did not discourage his mother. Revealing his talent for pyrotechnics, Ved Vyas thus says to his scribe Ganesha in a mock-heroic vein: "We Brahmin sons never deny our mothers, and we never fail to rise to these occasions. I rose and I came" (31). He took Ambika, Ambalika and a maid-servant of the former to bed on successive nights and this 'act of congress' amicably settled the 'issue of dynastic succession' (32). From Ambika's womb emerged blind Dhritarashtra, from Ambalika's pale Pandu while the maidservant gave birth to Vidur Dharmaputra who would one day be known for his wisdom.

Book II: *The Duel with the Crown*

This chapter describes the emergence of Ganga Datta/ Mahatma Gandhi as a national leader with radical ideas which began to worry the British rulers. Despite his 'personal eccentricities' (36) and fads like taking enemas and occasional pontifications on the virtues of sexual abstinence, Gangaji became gradually known as a formidable opponent of the foreign rule. He preached a lot about equality, justice and the right of the native people to decide their own fate. He spoke openly about *swaraj* or self-rule and pan-Indian nationalism and made Indians, in the face of the denigratory attitude of the colonizers to native languages and cultures (37), feel proud of their heritage. Ganga Datta was altogether different from other leaders of the time. A scion of the ruling class and caste, he waged a crusade against caste-distinctions. 'Not an easy man to place' (38), as Ronald Heaslop—the aide to British Resident in Hastinapur—described him, Gangaji taught others by setting personal examples. He believed in the power of moral authority and cleaned his own toilet 'to show that there is nothing inherently shameful about the task' (37). He considered untouchability a blot on Hinduism and declared it illegal in Hastinapur.

His preoccupation with larger ethical and political issues notwithstanding, Gangaji did not neglect his duties and responsibilities as a Regent. The unacknowledged sons of Ved Vyas grew up under Ganga's tutelage, 'as if they were his own children' (41). Although he himself became increasingly ascetic in his manners and life-style, Gangaji 'spared no extravaganza' in giving the boys best available education and material comfort. As a result, each of Ved Vyas's progeny developed into valuable assets to the country. Dhritarashtra, the blind son of Vichitravirya, 'found education in India a harrowing experience' and was sent to England where he acquired 'a formidable vocabulary and the vaguely abstracted manner of the over-educated' (41). With these assets he became 'a formidable debater, a Bachelor of Arts and a Fabian Socialist' (41). Pandu, his pale half-brother, was physically strong and had moral courage but what he lacked was judgement. He was expelled from one of the best colleges of the country for striking a British teacher, Prof. Kipling (Otten) who had denigrated the Indians and called them dogs. Vidur Dharmaputra, the son of Ambika's maidservant, outshone his brothers in both intellectual gifts and administrative ability. But since he knew from the beginning that he had no claim on the family throne, Vidur developed 'a sense of modesty and self-effacement' (42). He became a bureaucrat and joined the Indian Civil Service.

In course of time Gangaji arranged the marriages of his nephews and identified three suitable ladies for them. Dhritarashtra was married to Gandhari, a beautiful girl with lustrous eyes who hailed from a renowned family of Allahabad. She was rumoured to have received 'the boon of Lord Shiva to have no less than a hundred sons' (43). For Pandu he found two princesses, Kunti Yadab—widely known across the country for her scintillating beauty and a pre-marital scandal—and Madri who was not as glamorous as the former but completely unblemished. As a young girl, Kunti was believed to 'have conducted a brief and entirely unwise liaison with a certain Hyperion Helios, a foreign visitor at her father's palace' (44). The fruit of this indiscretion was a son whom she floated down the river in a reed basket to avoid public shame. For Vidur, Ganga found a young, elegant and convent-educated lady, the lithe daughter of a native king and his low-caste wife. Thus assuring the accession of his protégés to the throne of Hastinapur, Gangaji gave up the regency and retreated to a riverside *ashram* (Sabarmati) where he dedicated himself whole-heartedly to the cause of Truth and freedom.

The Great Indian Novel provides a concise and balanced portrait of Gangaji/Gandhiji with a view to reviving his memory among the people. Tharoor thinks that although Gandhi left behind a well-documented life, his countrymen have 'consigned him to the mists and myths of historical legend' so much so that he 'might as well have been a character from the *Mahabharata*' (47). The author believes that Indians have failed to relate the father of the nation to their lives not only because of the 'bastard educational institutions the British sired on us' (47) but also because of the prevailing political culture of the country after Independence in which the ruling elite promoted their own favourite politicians by pinning the ones they disliked to currency notes and concrete slabs. In this way Gandhi was effaced from the sphere of moral and cultural influence. In a bitter tone the narrator says: "Gangaji was the kind of person it is more convenient to forget . . . while he was alive, he was impossible to ignore; once he had gone, he was impossible to imitate" (47).

The Indian resistance against the British rule effectively began after the appearance of Ganga Datta at the helm of the Kaurava Party. The narrative delineates his role in awakening the masses against the colonizers by perfecting a system of non-violent struggle against their unjust exercise of power. It details the uniqueness of Gangaji's concept of Truth which he held dearer than his life: "No dictionary imbues the word with the depth of meaning Gangaji gave it. His truth emerged from his convictions: it meant not only what was accurate, but what was just and therefore right. Truth could not be obtained by 'untruthful,' or unjust, or violent means" (48). His first real experiment with truth came about in Motihari soon after he handed over the reins of Hastinapur to Dhritarashtra and Pandu. Documented in the history books as the Champaran Campaign, it was Gangaji's first 'duel with the crown.' The cause was the ineffable plight of indigo cultivators due to colonial exploitation:

> There was starvation in Motihari, not just because the land did not produce enough for its tillers to eat, but because it could not, under the colonialists' laws, be entirely devoted to keeping them alive. Three tenths of every man's land had to be consecrated to indigo . . . [which] had to be sold to British planters at a fixed price—fixed, that is, by the buyer. (50)

Gangaji sympathized with the plight of the helpless and starving peasants and announced his protest campaign. He toured the remote villages of the district, visited the huts of the poorest men to listen to their sufferings and held public meetings where the exploited farmers spoke for the first time about the inequity of their lives. The whole country saw 'the real heart of the new politics' and the whole world witnessed how 'a nation was rising, with a small, balding, semi-clad saint at its head' (51). Gangaji publicly defied the indigo-laws by removing an indigo plant and symbolically sowing a handful of wheat in its place. The

Motihari campaign pushed the British to the defensive and forced them to see Gangaji's point of view.

The most important aspect of this campaign was that it brought, for the first time, ordinary men and women into the mainstream of the freedom struggle. The poor and the middle classes 'got their place in the sun' and this broadening of mass base gave a new orientation to Indian nationalism. The Gangan concept of non-violent protest, which emerged from his convictions of justice, equality and liberty, also proved to be a timely and potent weapon in the fight against the British Raj: "Where sporadic terrorism and moderate constitutionalism had both proved ineffective, Ganga took the issue of freedom to the people as one of simple right and wrong—law versus conscience—and gave them a method to which the British had no response" (55). And it established him as the undisputed leader of the nationalist movement.

Book III: *The Rains Came*

The political fallout of Gangaji's Motihari campaign was the hasty annexation of Hastinapur to British India. While the father of the nation moved on relentlessly with a broader mission of fighting for the rights of the underprivileged and the exploited, Dhritarashtra and Pandu, who did not accompany their mentor in most of his politically strategic campaigns against the imperialists, were busy in Hastinapur ensuring their succession. As the book 'The Rains Came' shows, they were over-enthusiastic to perpetuate their hold on power through their progenies. In a deviation from the original, Gandhari mothered not one hundred sons but one girl daughter, Priya Duryodhani (who stands for Indira Gandhi). In order to fit the actual historical personages and events into the narrative design of the epic, the novelist makes such changes throughout the novel. Thus, Duryodhani with the altered sex represents one hundred Kauravas. The birth of Duryodhani is symbolically presented as something ominous. The narrator prepares the reader for a negative portrayal of

Duryodhani/Indira's character and anticipates her tyrannical rule through the use of well-conceived animal imagery:

> And then, from behind Gandhari's closed door just down the corridor, there emerged a single, long, wailing sound. We both stood transfixed. It was a baby's cry and yet it was more than that; it was a rare, sharp, high-pitched cry like that of a donkey in heat, and as it echoed around the house a sound started up outside as if in response, a weird animal moan, and then the sounds grew, as donkeys brayed in the distance, mares neighed in their pens, jackals howled in the forests, and through the cacophony we heard the beating of wings at the windows, the caw-caw-cawing of a cackle of crows, and penetrating through the shadows, the piercing shriek of the hooded vultures circling above the palace of Hastinapur. (73)

Dhritarashtra was disappointed at the birth of a girl child. But it was prophesied that this daughter would equal a thousand sons and that she would grow up to rule India one day.

Meanwhile Pandu's sexual excess in the company of two young wives resulted in a near fatal accident. He recovered somehow and was compelled to give up the 'pleasures of the flesh' (66). He went to Gangaji's riverside ashram and began to learn politics and Gangan philosophy. His transformation under his mentor's tutelage was remarkable: "In discourse his speech became erudite, his tone measured. In debate he thought high and aimed low. He became adept at religion, generous in philanthropy and calm in continence" (69). But he remained eager as before to have sons. This anxiety for an heir led him to secure the tacit approval of his wives for having progenies through extramarital relationships.

Book IV: *A Raj Quartet*

While 'The Duel with the Crown' demonstrates the manner in which Ganga Datta sharpened the weapons of morality, truth and non-violent resistance to encounter the brute force of colonialism, 'A Raj Quartet' shows his determination to persist with them in the face of opposition. The official announcement of

Hastinapur's annexation met with a sense of outrage and a vociferous protest on the part of its citizens. As the news spread that Gangaji would address a mass rally to denounce the imperialist design, people—irrespective of class, caste and age—began to flock to the historic Bibigarh Gardens (Jallianwala Bagh). Apprehending trouble, the British Resident called the army. Colonel Rudyard (who reminds one of the colonialist writer Rudyard Kipling but actually stands for Brigadier Reginald Dyer) was ordered to prevent the unlawful assembly. Rudyard's soldiers opened fire indiscriminately, killing hundreds of unarmed men, women and children. The Bibigarh massacre—so called to parody the Bibigarh rape in Paul Scott's Raj fiction *The Day of the Scorpion*—is a fictional representation of the Jallianwala Bagh massacre and Tharoor's cool, ironic description of the scene only matches the spirit of its presentation in Salman Rushdie's *Midnight's Children*:

> They loaded and fired their rifles coldly, clinically, without haste or passion or sweat or anger, resting their weapons against the tops of the brick walls . . . and emptying their magazines into the human beings before them with trained precision. I have often wondered whether they heard the screams of the crowd, Ganapathi, whether they noticed the blood, and the anguished wails of the women, and the stampeding of the trampling feet as panic-stricken villagers sought to get away from the sudden hail of death raining remorselessly down upon them. . . . I think of the Bibigarh Gardens Massacre as a frozen tableau from a silent film, black and white and mute, an Indian *Guernica*. (80-81)

The callous remark passed by Rudyard on receiving the figures of people dead and injured—"Only 84 bullets wasted. . . . Not bad" (81)—reminds one of the Brigadier Dyer's words in Rushdie's novel: "Good shooting . . . we have done a jolly good thing" (36). It reveals the brutality of the colonizers and their total lack of human feelings. In a sharp and laconic comment, the narrator unveils the inhumanity of the colonial ethics and the hollowness of the claim of carrying on a civilizing mission in the underdeveloped and backward countries made by the cohorts of the colonizers:

> Or perhaps [Rudyard] just acted in the way dictated by the simple logic of colonialism, under which the rules of humanity applied only to the rulers, for the rulers were people and the people were objects. Objects to be controlled, disciplined, kept in their place and taught lessons like so many animals: yes, the civilizing mission upon which Rudyard and his tribe were embarked made savages of all of us, and all of them. (80)

The Bibigarh Gardensmassacre, which crystallized the worst aspect of colonialism, not only confirmed the wisdom of Ganga Datta and the justification of his principles of Truth and non-violence but also served to unite the entire nation to challenge the might of the evil empire.

In the wake of Bibigarh Gardens massacre Dhritarashtra and Pandu joined the nationalist cause whole-heartedly. Dhritarashtra's disappointment with a girl child and the declining health of his wife led him to politics. But his flair for the job surprised everybody and before long he became 'a leading light of the Kaurava Party' (85). Tharoor's narrative gives an extremely negative estimate of Dhritarashtra's/Nehru's ability as a leader of the Kaurava/Congress organization. His role in both pre and post independence Indian politics is suggested by the allegorical frame. As Dhritarashtra he is Gandhi's 'blind' and visionary disciple and his blindness is used to a satirical effect: 'He had the blind man's gift of seeing the world not as it was, but as he wanted it to be' (85). It made him completely out of touch with the reality around him. Tharoor also suggests that Nehru gained importance in the party and succeeded in controlling the reins of power after independence because of the blessings of Gandhi who 'made no secret of his preference for the slim and confident young man' (85).

In contrast, Pandu/Subhas Bose is presented as a more pragmatic character: 'Not for Pandu the flights of fancy of his sightless sibling, nor, for that matter, the ideological flirtations. .

. . Pandu believed in taking stock of reality' (85). Pandu's role as the party's chief organizer brought into sharp focus his political differences with his blind brother: 'The process of building up a party structure and a cadre committed to run it in the teeth of colonial hostility convinced him that discipline and organization were far greater virtues than ideals and doctrines. It was the classic distortion . . . to which our late leader would herself one day fall prey, the elevation of means over ends, of methods over aspirations' (86). This incompatibility between means and ends continued to dog the two leaders. It was harnessed successfully as long as Gangaji was in charge of the party's affairs. But with the slackening of his grip, the differences revealed themselves leading to an irremediable rift between the two brothers.

Gangaji not only spearheaded the national struggle against colonial rule but also nurtured the Kaurava Party as a nursery of would-be leaders. As Ved Vyas remarks humorously: "We were to develop a pluralist system, so a plurality of leaders had to be born to run it" (86). The country's third generation of leadership was ensured not only by Gandhari through her travail but also by Pandu's wives, Kunti and Madri, through their post-marital liaison approved and arranged by their husband himself. Out of Kunti's extra-marital congress with Justice Dharma, Major Vayu, and Devendra Yogi were born Yudhishtir, Bhim and Arjun respectively, while Madri seduced a pair of identical twins who gave her two sons, Nakul and Sahadev. But the jubilation over the engineered birth of Pandu's sons did not last long. The whole issue of 'heir-conditioning' (89) was rendered redundant by the annexation of Hastinapur by the British.

Book V: *The Powers of Silence*

While Dhritarashtra and Pandu remained busy ensuring their succession to the throne of Hastinapur through their progeny, Ganga Datta moved on untiringly from one corner of the country to another with a broader mission of fighting against the evils of colonial rule and for the rights of the exploited and the underprivileged. After the overwhelming success of Motihari campaign, Budge Budge in Bengal became his destination where he tested the strength of his truth force and of the weapon of moral war against the foreigners. What brought Ganga to the Bengali town on the banks of the river Hooghly was the exploitation of the indigenous jute-factory workers by Scottish mill-owners.

As a part of its anti-colonial discourse, Tharoor's novel highlights the exploitative aspect of the British rule in India and its pernicious effect on the country's economy: "the British killed the Indian artisan, they created the Indian 'landless labourer,' they exported our full employment and they invented our poverty" (95). The narrative takes note of the Indian weavers whose thumbs had been cut off by the British in order to protect the machines of Lancashire and of the native peasants whose lands were handed over to the zamindars who guaranteed the imperialists the much-needed social peace to run the country. It chronicles the loot of the country's fabulous wealth by the foreign merchants and traders who 'took what they could take, leaving Indians to wallow in their leavings' (95).

Gangaji was moved to pity by the ineffable plight of the locked-out workers, who were demanding a slight increase in their wages, and he took up their cause. He was joined in this humanitarian mission by the enlightened and idealistic sister of a jute-mill owner, named suggestively Sarah Moore. When the persuasion of this unlikely duo failed to move the intransigent mill-owners, Gangaji decided to fast unto death to achieve his objective. The reaction of the starving workers to the declaration of this unheard-of method of fighting for justice was astounding: "A great collective sigh escaped the lips of the crowd, like the first puff of a restive volcano; then a silence descended upon the throng as every man and woman . . . strained to catch Gangaji's next words" (101). Gangaji's fast nearly stopped the heartbeat of the nation and terribly frightened the British authority in India that compelled the mill-owners to give in to the workers' demand. Ganga Datta won his battle against injustice through a unique means and with it he won the adulation of the country. This was the first time Ganga/Gandhi directed his non-violence not against his enemy but against himself. He startled the world by showing how far he could go to defend what he considered to be right and just. This principled stand gave a new dimension to Indian nationalism: "Indian nationalism had generated its share of agitators, boycotters and bonfire-stokers; its leaders had resorted to legal texts, holy sacraments and bombs; but no one had ever before tried to starve himself to death" (101).

The reward of the Budge Budge campaign was three-fold: (a) Ganga found in Sarah Moore, who understood him 'intuitively' (102), his future disciple; (b) he widened the mass-base of Indian nationalism by including the most neglected section of the people—the poor and the lower middle class—into the mainstream politics and giving their due place under the sun; and (c) he discovered the strength of his convictions and the potential of fasting as a moral weapon in his struggle against colonialism. The lesson he learnt in this protest campaign was that 'the best way to bring his principles to life was, paradoxically, by being prepared to die for them' (105). This realization proved, according to Tharoor, to be the ultimate strength of the freedom movement. Gangaji's willingness to lay down his life for the nation 'set the tone for the other sacrifices that were, eventually, to make freedom possible' (105).

Book VI: *Forbidden Fruit*

It is interesting to note that the two disciples of Gangaji, Dhritarashtra and Pandu, did not feature in the two important episodes of his political career narrated so far. The reason was very obvious: they were not there at that time. But to say that will be considered blasphemous by the blind followers of these Hastinapuri princelings who believe, like many post-independence hagiographers, that their heroes followed Ganga Datta at every step during the freedom struggle. Ved Vyas's narrative emphatically says that they did not, and that 'most of the crucial events in Gangaji's life and career were those in which he acted alone, resolving the dictates of his hyperactive conscience within, and by, himself' (109).

This leads him to digress and make some perceptive observations about historical discourse and the nature of historical process. Tharoor holds the view that the making of history, like India's struggle against colonial rule and achievement of independence, is a collective effort, involving thousands of nondescript people. But when it is shaped into a written account, many of these participants are left out. This problem is inherent in the very process of composing history into an ordered and understandable account. He admits that the persons and events which are left out in any ordered narrative of the past may not necessarily be of lesser importance than the ones which are included. The protagonists of his story comprise a 'little band of individuals and families selected from the swirling mists of an old man's memory to represent a past in which others too have played a significant but unrecalled part' (110). The last observation highlights the principles of selectivity and choice exercised by a historian in the recounting of the past which is seldom a disinterested enterprise, and points out the fact that Ved Vyas's version of India's colonial as well as postcolonial history is shaped by his faltering memory. It is 'memory's truth,' as Saleem Sinai called his version in *Midnight's Children*, but it is valid like any other version.

While Gangaji was engaged in his single-minded quest for developing a close rapport with the masses of India and symbolizing their cause through identification with their suffering, Dhritarashtra and Pandu were assiduously working 'to organize and promote . . . the institution that would one day propel Gangaji's vision into a tangible nationhood—the Kaurava Party' (110). Before the advent of Ganga Datta in the national politics, the party had been 'a distinguished but remarkably ineffective forum for the rhetorical articulation of Anglophile dissatisfaction with the English' (110). But Ganga's unorthodox methods and their spectacular success changed everything. The Gangan politics shook up 'the sterile verities of the party's past and opened it up for capture' (111). The Hastinapur princelings joined politics when the whole country was thus swayed by the Gangan whirlwind.

Dhritarashtra, who had returned from England with 'traces of the right accent along with streaks of the wrong ideas' (111), soon captured the 'ideological heights' of the Kaurava organization. From the beginning, Gangaji made his preference for his blind protégé very clear: 'The Kauravas were left in no doubt that Dhritarashtra was Gangaji's man' (111). Initially, however, he indulged Dhritarashtra but relied on his pale nephew, Pandu. They worked in tandem to implement Gangaji's policies: "It was Pandu who took the party banners into the most remote villages, while Dhritarashtra toured the lecture halls and the meeting rooms of urban India" (111-12). The division of labour was sanctified by Gangaji himself. But Ved Vyas's memoir takes note of the lop-sided portrayal of Dhritarashtra's/Nehru's role during this crucial period of the country's freedom struggle by official hagiographers. Tharoor is particularly critical of the role of Priya Duryodhani (Indira Gandhi) in inflating her father's contribution at the cost of Pandu (Subhas Bose) to whom, the narrator admits, injustice was done:

> When, years later, Duryodhani spoke darkly of the immense and unrivalled sacrifices her father and she had made for the nation, I would think of poor Pandu, by then long turned to ash and almost forgotten. . . . And I would muse, Ganapathi, on the injustices of Fate. (112)

In view of the incompatibility of the two leaders and the insurmountable differences of their attitudes, the separation between them was inevitable. The narrator correctly analyses the reasons why the brothers fell apart: "I watched them both, my flawed, gifted sons . . . and I saw the inevitability of their separation. Pandu became impatient of Dhritarashtra's oratorical certitudes, his lofty convictions and vaulting ambition. Dhritarashtra, in turn, had little time for Pandu's atavistic traditionalism, his political earthiness" (112). Gangaji was aware of the growing disaffection between his two most illustrious disciples but he did nothing to heal the rift.

The differences between the two Kaurava stalwarts became increasingly visible, with Pandu beginning to take positions at variance with his elder brother's. He constantly insisted on adopting a harder line against the British than the organization—whose strategy was guided by 'Gangaji's wisdom and Dhritarashtra's cunning' (113)—was willing to adopt. Gangaji's open preference for Dhritarashtra and undisguised vindication of his stand on all major political issues further alienated Pandu.

The disagreement between the two came out into the open over the issue of sending a Kaurava delegation to the Round Table Conference convened by the British in London to discuss the future of India. Pandu vehemently argued against sending a delegation as he viewed the whole thing as a sinister imperialistic ploy to divide the Indians and weaken the nationalist movement. But once again he was disregarded and the Kaurava working committee, 'at Dhritarashtra's glib urging, agreed not only to attend but to send Gangaji as the party's sole representative to the conference' (115). The failure of the 'circular and circumlocutious' talk only proved the prescience of Pandu.

If the decision to send Gangaji to the Round Table Conference reflected the arrogance of Dhritarashtra, the incontrovertible success of the Mango March ('Forbidden Fruit'), a parodic representation of the historic Salt March, evinced the solecism of Pandu.

In conformity with their unjust policy of exploitation, the British colonial administrators—described by the narrator as 'pompous mediocrity' (116)—decided to impose a tax on the mango, the only luxury which the Indian masses, irrespective of their class, caste and creed, could afford: 'the colonial regime had decided that the mango too had to earn its keep. Mangoes were a cash crop; accordingly a tax was to be levied on the fruit. . . . The days of the free munch were over' (117). The colonial announcement was received by the people with 'stunned disbelief' and 'collective howls of outrage' (117). As a leader of the masses, Gangaji heard their protest and sensed in it a cause. He wrote a letter to the viceroy announcing his decision to embark upon a non-violent satyagraha to resist and defy the mango tax. Pandu was aghast at the decision which, he felt, would only trivialize the cause of freedom. But Gangaji stuck to his resolution and advised his pale protégé to trust his wisdom. Before embarking on the famous Mango March which fired the people's imagination and stirred their hearts as few movements before had ever done, Ganga Datta officially anointed Dhritarashtra as his successor. This decision completely alienated Pandu from his preceptor. Enraged by Gangaji's favouritism, he walked out of his ashram, never to return.

The narrative emphasizes the fact that despite the quaintness in Gangaji's style of functioning, he was a great strategist, and that, though there was a lot of theatricality in his social and political campaigns, he gave the freedom movement a much-needed publicity both in India and abroad. As a result, the people of the country were convinced that they were led not by a saint but by a pragmatic politician whose feet remained firmly on the ground. In order to inflate the issue of the mango march to one of national importance and keep it in the news for long, Gangaji undertook a 288-mile march from his ashram to the grove of a sympathetic landlord to violate the infamous act which had turned mango into a 'forbidden fruit.' His penchant for theatrics, exploited by the narrator to great comic effect, succeeded in transforming this apparently trivial issue into a major cause of protest against colonialism. With thousands of volunteers and reporters in tow, Ganga Datta reached the mango grove and plucked from a tree the first fruit of the country's liberation. He was arrested by the police but not before he made his point.

Unfortunately the peaceful agitation, which exposed the colonialists and held them up to ridicule, turned violent in a place called Chaurasta (Chauri Chaura). It led to the death of some policemen and the abrupt suspension by an aggrieved Ganga of the most successful movement of mass civil disobedience in British India. Many people, including Pandu, termed the move as an act of betrayal. In a meeting of the leading members of the Kaurava Party, he gave vent to his annoyance with his mentor: "That's what's wrong with our entire way of running this party. Is this a Kaurava movement, or a one-man show?" (126) Ved Vyas, the eldest member of the party, tried to explain that to Gangaji the principle of non-violence was more important than the success of any single agitation, and that this new weapon would be blunted if the people resorted to the old weapon of violence. But his words failed to convince Pandu and silence his dissenting voice:

> Dissent, Ganapathi, is like a Gurkha's *kukri*: once it emerges from its sheath it must draw blood before it can be put away again. I knew that blood would inevitably have to be drawn, and I felt the pain of the knife already, knowing that it was my blood that coursed through the veins of both potential victims: my blind son and my pale son, condemned to fight on history's battlefield. (127)

Book VII: *The Son Also Rises*

As the struggle for freedom gathered momentum under the dynamic leadership of Ganga Datta, the cause of the Muslim Group (League) led by Mohammed Ali Karna (Jinnah) began to weaken this nationalist resurgence at the instigation of the imperialists. Shashi Tharoor's version of India's colonial history provides an insightful analysis of the communal issue which led to the partition of the country. According to Tharoor, the Muslim Group was a creation of the sinister colonial policy of 'divide and rule.' As he says, "The Muslims of India were no more cohesive and monolithic a group than any other in the country. Until politics intervened Indians simply accepted that people were all sorts of different things" (133). These differences were an intrinsic aspect of Indian life whose guiding credo was 'unity in diversity.'

In Tharoor's view, religious differences did not necessarily imply hostility. There had been, in the country's long political history, always 'a high degree of constructive interaction among . . . various communities' (134). Indians had never politicized their social differences and religion had little to do with their national politics. It was the British rule which sowed the seeds of division among different communities. As the narrator observes bitterly: "It was British civil serpent who made our people collectively bite the apple of discord" (134). Terrified by the revolt of Indian sepoys in 1857, the British policy-makers rediscovered the importance of the Latin adage: 'Divide et impera' and decided to drive wedges between Indians. Severely criticizing this divisive strategy which would have far-reaching consequences in the subsequent history of the subcontinent, the narrator says, "The strategy was amoral, the tactics immoral. The obvious cleavage to strike upon was between 'the Hindus' and 'the Muslims.' It mattered little that such terms themselves (concealing as they did so many complex divisions and identities) made little sense, nor that they covered groups which had never, in all of India's political history, functioned as monoliths. It mattered little, because Indians proved only too willing to echo Britain's political illiteracy and agree to be defined in terms imposed upon them by their conquerors" (135).

As a part of this policy, the British created separate Muslim electorate and encouraged an assorted group of puppets to start a political association of the Muslims—the Muslim Group. The members of this Group received British titles and funds and they were led by an 'overweight sybarite' named Gaga Shah (Aga Khan). The self-appointed leaders of the Group, who 'tripped over themselves to protest their undying loyalty to the British Raj' (136), could not win the respect of the Muslim masses who looked upon them as British stooges. As a result, the most serious Muslim politicians, like their counterparts in Christian and Parsi communities, supported Ganga Datta's Kaurava Party. It is at this stage, Mohammed Ali Karna emerged on the national political scene and became, before long, a leading light of the Kaurava organization.

Mohammed Ali Jinnah, the modern Karna, is one of the most interesting characters of *The Great Indian Novel*. Tharoor goes into the details of the circumstances of his birth, the reasons of his alienation from the Indian National Congress which made him join the Muslim League and demand for a separate Islamic state, in order to establish a parallelism between the mythical Karna and his modern prototype. The fruit of Kunti's adolescent error, whom she had floated on the river to avoid scandal, and the adopted son of a rich man's driver, Karna joined the Kaurava Party after his return from London to set up an exceptionally successful practice as a barrister in the Bombay High Court. A star of the Inner Temple, he dazzled the nation with the brilliance of his appearance, intellect and speech. He had great poise and confidence which were 'matched by his forensic skill' (137). All sorts of myths were built up around this young man who, despite his secular upbringing, was destined to be the defender of Islam.

Karna's alienation from the mainstream of Indian politics was largely due to the fact that his view of the nationalist cause was completely different from that of Ganga Datta. Karna approached politics as a lawyer with a clinical perception about the British system and he had a deep-seated prejudice against the masses. Analyzing his difference from the other Kaurava leaders, the narrator remarks, "It was as a skilled advocate of a constitutional brief that Karna approached his politics. Not for him the sweaty trudges through the *mofussil* districts, the mass rallies that Gangaji addressed in one or another vernacular; Karna, always elegant and well-groomed, was comfortable only in the language of his education and in the kind of surroundings in which he had acquired it" (137). He was isolated in the Kaurava party due to his egotism and arrogance which would not allow him to accept a subordinate role in the organization dominated by Gangaji and his disciples.

Karna's reservations about Hinduism were also responsible for his gradual disaffection with Ganga Datta's party. Tharoor's narrative holds Gangaji/Gandhiji responsible for Karna's/Jinnah's separation from the nationalist cause. Karna, according to Tharoor, had never had a communal mindset. He was secular, rational and modern. He hated Islamic fundamentalism and even developed an un-Islamic taste for Scotch and cocktail sausages. What separated Karna from Gangaji was, therefore, not Islam but the latter's fetish about Hinduism. Because of his deep-rooted grounding in Hindu ethos, Ganga/ Gandhi consistently exploited the Hindu religious symbols to mobilize the Indian masses and galvanize them against the colonial rule. And this, Tharoor believes like many contemporary historians, made the nationalist leaders of other communities apprehensive about the threat of growing Hindu influence to their identities and, therefore, led to their isolation. Ved Vyas narrates Karna's dislike for Gandhi thus:

> Karna was not much of a Muslim but he found Gangaji too much of a Hindu. The Mahaguru's traditional attire, his spiritualism, his spouting of the ancient texts, his ashram, his constant harking back to an idealized pre-British past that Karna did not believe in (and was impatient with)—all this made the young man mistrustful of the Great Teacher. (142)

Gangaji's Hindu rhetoric to foment the Indian people against the foreign rule made him suspicious. He found the Kaurava Party under Gangaji's leadership 'insufficiently secular' and this, in turn, made him more 'consciously Muslim' (142). What is surprising, even ironical, is that a man like Gandhi, who struggled all his life for Hindu-Muslim amity and even died of bullets from a Hindu fanatic for his supposed love, and preference, for the Muslims, should be held responsible for encouraging Muslim separatism in the country. But this view is implicit in Tharoor's interpretation of Gandhi's politics.

Karna's separation from the Kauravas came in the wake of the failure of the Round Table Conference, after his meeting with the head of the Muslim Group, Gaga Shah, in London. The meeting increased the distance between him and Ganga Datta. Though he viewed Gangaji and the Kaurava Party as 'the only actors of any consequence,' he believed them to be standing for 'all that is retrogressive and populist in Indian politics' (145). It was not that he had any respect for the Muslim Group which was 'a moribund . . . gathering of nawabs and zamindars' (145). But of all the available political alternatives in India, this was the only organization which enjoyed a certain amount of prestige in the eyes of the British and had the best potential. He accepted the leadership of the Muslim Group and, on his return to India, became its all-powerful President. Within years, his able leadership and the favours of the colonial rulers turned the Group into a serious contender for power: "it was now a nationalist movement in its own right, like the Kaurava Party. The only difference was that the Group considered nationalism to be divisible. 'Independence without Hindu domination' was Karna's new slogan" (148). Gangaji's party, riven by dissent and internecine conflict, could not meet the challenge posed by the decisively led Muslim Group.

Book VIII: *Midnight's Parents*

The novel incorporates a good number of incidents from the epic which are not necessary for its historical design. The training of the five Pandava brothers under the tutorship of Drona and the private lives of Dhritarashtra's neglected wife and lonely daughter have little to do with the historical narrative. But the author has included these scenes and incidents in order to give the story the magnitude and the digressive quality of the original.

The bearded socialist Jayaprakash Drona (who stands for Jayaprakash Narayan) is presented here as a Brahmin versed in the great tradition of Sanskritic learning. A roving sage, he had once come across an English civil servant named Ronald Heaslop (Tharoor's postcolonial version of Ronny Heaslop, the typical colonist in E.M. Forster's *A Passage to India*). Over a period of time Drona imparted his knowledge of the 'ancient practices and customs' (159) of the country to the inquisitive Englishman. Some sort of intimacy developed between the two and, at the time of leave-taking, the grateful British official admitted that he owed his knowledge of India and her culture to the sage. He even gave the Brahmin his personal card and requested him to visit his residence if he ever needed any help.

Years later, Drona, now a married man with a young child named Ashwathaman, was in search of a patron for his son. He remembered the request of Heaslop and went to meet him. The experience he gathered during that ill-fated encounter completely disillusioned Drona of British civility and gave him a bitter taste of the colonial relationship. At first Heaslop refused to recognize him. Even when he did, as Drona produced his card and reminded him of their earlier friendship, his behaviour was rude and it smacked of colonial prejudice. Heaslop told the sage that there was no knowledge which the Indians could instruct the British people in, and that all he had received from the Brahmin was 'superstitious twaddle' (160). Echoing his earlier avatar in Forster's novel, the despicable colonist said to the dumbfounded Indian: "Don't be stupid. We are not here to be your friends, black man; we are here to rule you. There is no friendship possible in this world between the likes of you and such as me; not now, not here, not yet, not ever" (161). Out of a sense of charity the British national offered him some small coins which he scornfully refused. The humiliated Brahmin took a solemn vow to work actively for the end of the colonial rule by not only supporting the Kaurava Party in its struggle against the British but also 'by educating and training those who will one day rise to lead our people when we replace the alien system they have thrust upon us' (161). He was appointed by Gangaji as a tutor of the Pandava brothers and he began to train them on a variety of subjects ranging from dialectics to diuretics.

In course of time Yudhishtir, who excelled in his studies, showed an inclination for legal career. Bhim, who was held in dread by all for his exceptional musculature, became the self-appointed protector of his brothers. Arjun turned out to be the perfect student who 'united all the opposite virtues of human nature: he was prince and commoner, brain and brawn' (151). The twins of Madri—Nakul and Sahadev—did not lag behind their half-brothers. They turned into the right foils for their extraordinarily talented elders.

While Pandu's sons were thus engaged in absorbing lessons from Drona, Priya Duryodhani grew up into a frail but beautiful girl in the lonely quarters of their palatial home, with none but her perennially sick mother to give her company. Gandhari, who was betrayed by her destiny in both the number and the gender of her progeny, simply 'wasted away in the home she had hoped to make with her perennially absent husband' (152). She had sacrificed her most precious possession—by way of blindfolding her large eyes—for Dhritarashtra but her blind husband was not there to share the darkness with her. He could not forgive Gandhari for delivering a girl child and, away from home, he addressed all his letters not to his long-suffering wife but to his daughter. Duryodhani silently watched her mother becoming more and more withdrawn and grim as her health deteriorated. The exposure to the betrayal of her mother's exceptional sacrifice left a lasting impression on Duryodhani who would never, in her life, be able to trust any human being, not even her father. The episode of Duryodhani's juvenile attempt to kill Bhim (152-53) has nothing to do with the historical design of the narrative but it gives an early hint of Dhritarashtra's scheming daughter who could go to any length to do away with her political opponents and who 'acted only according to the dictates of her own conscienceless mind' (155).

The thread of the historical narrative is picked up again to describe the nationalist movement which had reached a critical juncture as the parents of the impending midnight found themselves at crossroads. Karna rose dramatically to national stature and established himself as the undisputed leader of the Muslim Group. Gangaji, advanced in age now and already turned into a 'global legend' (165), began to teach more and more about love, peace and brotherhood. He had left the leadership of the Kaurava Party to his blind political heir, Dhritarashtra, and devoted himself to the espousal of the moral and spiritual values which informed his politics.

Ganga Datta's unabashed partiality towards Dhritarashtra and his method of directing the nationalist movement, particularly his abrupt suspension of the most successful campaign of civil disobedience—the Mango March—led disgruntled Pandu to break ranks and revolt against his mentor. With a view to giving a new direction to the movement and making it more action-oriented, Ved Vyas's pale son announced his candidature for the presidency of the Kaurava Party. Not prepared to accommodate dissent in the organization and let Pandu get away with it, Gangaji put up his own candidate for the election, a lesser known untouchable (Pattavi Sitaramaiya). Thus the Party faced the first major challenge, since its inception, to its leadership due to the revolt of a man whose victory might have changed the course of Indian history.

While Gangaji was finding ways to meet the challenge of his pale disciple, his blind protégé began to wait patiently—at Ganga's advice—for the premiership of the first national government whose formation was not, after the passage of the Government of India Act by the British Parliament, an impossible dream any longer.

Book IX: *Him—Or, The Far Power-Villain*

The title of this chapter is a parody of M.M. Kaye's Raj fiction, *The Far Pavillions*. The narrative here dwells on the vicissitudes of Pandu's/Subhas Bose's career vis-à-vis his relationship with Gangaji/Gandhiji. It is made clear that Pandu lost the race for the leadership of the Kaurava Party because of Gangaji's undisguised preference for Dhritarashtra. The narrator praises his efforts in the cause of the country's freedom but also explains how he perished because of his quixotic dreams and lack of judgement.

Pandu carried on an aggressive campaign among the rank and file of the Kaurava Party. The dedicated Kaurava workers, who organized the party at the grass-root level, could easily identify themselves with Pandu's cause. In him they found a true representative of the masses. The leadership of the Kaurava organization had remained, even after the advent of Ganga Datta at the helm, reserved for the educated, articulate and wealthy section of the Indian society. Even Gangaji, who had widened the Party's support and given it a mass base, did very little to alter the pattern at the top where a handful always reigned. So in the first democratic election in the Party, Pandu defeated Gangaji's handpicked candidate and became 'the first President of the plebeians' (171). Never tolerant of divisiveness, Ganga Datta could not accept Pandu's victory which 'posed a threat' (172) to his own position as the supreme leader of the Party. He brought immense moral pressure on Pandu through unremitting correspondences, public outcry, press release and systematic campaigns within the Party, thus forcing him to resign.

An aggrieved Pandu wrote a letter to his former mentor requesting him to dissociate himself from the dissident activities of his own supporters. Gangaji refused to oblige his rebellious nephew on the ground that he could not 'advise faithful servants of the Kaurava cause against acting according to the dictates of their consciences' (174). Abandoned by his preceptor and cornered within the Party, Pandu sought a vote of confidence from the Kaurava Working Committee and lost. In utter despair he resigned. Thus, Ganga Datta, the 'paragon' of Truth, justice and righteousness, forced his insubordinate disciple out of the race for power.

Tharoor's narrative, which demythologizes and debunks historical characters over whom a mythical aura has been spread by hagiographers, is highly critical of Gandhiji's role in the expulsion of Subhas Bose from the Congress Party. It demonstrates the Great Soul's reservations about dissent and his unwillingness to accommodate decisions other than what he wanted or liked. He became synonymous with the Party and disapproved plurality of views. The very fact that Gandhiji had the last say in the affairs of the Congress alienated many talented and promising leaders like Subhas and prevented true democracy from taking roots—an eventuality which would have far-reaching consequences for this nationalist organization.

The rest of the chapter breaks into verse (it is written in quatrains rhyming a b a b) to follow the pathetic destiny of Pandu/ Subhas which is unravelled in a bathetic form. Once again irony becomes a mode of perception and it is evident in the parodic tone adopted by the narrator: "'Away with Tolstoy,

Ruskin, Buddha:/ Their ideas just make little men litter./ No more 'truth-force,' only *yuddha*-/ It's time to learn from that chap Hitler.'" (177). The chapter follows the well-known historical account of Subhas Bose's escape from the country during the World War II and his arrival in Germany, via Afghanistan, to seek the help of the axis power—comprising Germany, Italy and Japan—for the country's cause:

> Oh, he'd flirted, it's true, with Fascist ideas,
> But those didn't count in the end;
> As he'd said to his wives, 'It's simply, my dears,
> That my enemy's enemy's my friend. (180-81)

In Tharoor's version, Subhas Chandra's years of exile were a great waste ('futile, absurd' [182]). He was virtually betrayed by the foreign powers whose assistance he actively sought. Hitler's Germany gave Subhas/ Pandu, who asked for weapons to fight against the British, only the permission to make speeches for his countrymen on 'Deutsche Welle.' The Japanese, in the meantime, had demolished the imperial myth of Britain's military supremacy. Parodying Kipling, the narrator says, "(In fact, Ganapathi, if truth be told/ The bloody 'white man's burden'/ Was what our coolies—cudgelled, cajoled—/ Bore on their heads and cursed in.)" (182). With the defeat and shameful retreat of the British army, "Hope dawned in Indian hearts and laps/ That we too could win Independence" (182). Pandu arrived in Singapore from Berlin and with Japanese help formed the Indian National Army which consisted mainly of Indian 'P.O. double-yous.' He inspired the demoralized soldiers with the dream of freedom and infused them with nationalist pride. But Tharoor deviates from the known historical account by suggesting that Subhas/ Pandu was let down by the Japanese who did not allow the I.N.A. to fight against the British since they could not rely on the ex-POWs whom they regarded as traitors. However, the fortunes of the war were soon turned, and the British offensive began.

The beleaguered Japanese now gave Pandu's army the much-awaited chance to fight. But, as Tharoor's narrative puts it, "the going got rough,/And his war-weary *sainiks*, unable to advance,/ Found Pandu's slogans no longer enough" (187). Under British firing, they forgot his 'eloquent charms' and 'fled, or simply surrendered' (187). The Japanese ordered Pandu to leave Singapore in a plane which crashed in mid-air, killing the defeated and dejected Indian hero. The lurid details of the Pandu-Madri love scene on board the ill-fated plane, in which the tragic hero of India's freedom struggle died just at the moment he was about to reach the greatest sexual climax of his life, are not only grotesque and defamatory but also extraneous to the main course of historical events in the novel. Pandu's death was deeply mourned by his countrymen, most vociferously by his blind half-brother, Dhritarashtra.

Book X: *Darkness at Dawn*

The title of this episode is reminiscent of Arthur Koestler's celebrated novel, *Darkness at Noon*. The chapter begins with an account of Duryodhani's neglected childhood spent at the bedside of her sick mother, who is sinking 'inexorably into another world' (195), and the training of the Pandava brothers under the tutorship of their socialist teacher, Jayaprakash Drona. The account follows the mythological narrative with some points of departure, the most remarkable one being the episode of Ekalavya. Ekalavya, the son of a maidservant, eavesdropped while Drona taught his pupils and emulated his best student, Arjun. An irate Drona chastised the poor but brilliant boy and asked for a fee: the thumb of his right hand. But the modern Ekalavya, 'a free-loader,' refused to pay it.

The historical narrative resumes amidst elections to the provincial governments—the first under the Government of India Act. Gangaji's Kaurava Party swept the polls and his Muslim followers won most of the reserved constituencies defeating Muslim Group candidates. Karna swallowed the galling defeat and, as a political strategy, proposed to join the Kauravas in coalition governments. But Ganga Datta's Party refused, under pressure from the Kaurava Muslim leaders like Mohammed Rafi

(Maulana Abul Kalam Azad), to enter into any coalition with Karna's Group. The political fall-out of the Kaurava decision was direct confrontation with the Muslim Group. In a meeting of the party elders, Karna declared war against his political opponents: 'As far as the Kauravas are concerned, gentlemen, it is war' (201).

Meanwhile the British had declared war against Nazi Germany in the wake of Hitler's aggression in Poland. They involved India in their war efforts without consulting the elected representatives of the people. Insulted and humiliated, Gangaji's followers resigned en bloc, ignoring the advice of Vidur against such precipitate action. The decision proved counter-productive. It weakened the Kaurava support base because they were no longer in a position to dole out patronage. With the help of the British, the Muslim Group formed minority governments in the provinces and set about increasing their following systematically. Thus reduced to a position of irrelevance, the frustrated Kauravas met under the chairmanship of Ganga Datta and, in what is described by Tharoor as 'a desperate and not entirely well-thought-out bid to regain the political limelight' (206), declared a new campaign of civil disobedience: 'Quit India.' The clarion call of Gangaji captured the people's imagination and the magic words spread across the country like 'the heartbeat of a national awakening' (206). But the rebellion was nipped in the bud as the British police arrested the prominent leaders within hours of the 'Quit India' call.

With the consolidation of the Muslim Group hold on Indian politics, the demand for Karnistan (literally 'the Hacked-off Land,' a separate Muslim state) became more strident. In Tharoor's view, this 'Islamic Utopia' would be simultaneously 'a tribute to its eponymous founder and an advertisement for its proponents' physical political intent' (207).

While Karna, who was popularly known as 'Khalifa-e-Mashriq,' posed a serious threat to 'what Gangaji stood for politically' (208), another person, a slight, embittered figure, began to bide her time to commit the most heinous act of retribution in the 20th century history of India. Amba, the princess of Kashi whose life had been thoughtlessly destroyed by her well-intentioned abductor, was almost ready to exact her revenge on Gangaji. After years of meditation, prayers and austerities, she had pleased Lord Shiva and come to learn from the god the secret to destroy the destroyer of her nuptial bliss: "Ganga Datta will only leave this world when he no longer wishes to remain in it. When such a moment comes, he can be destroyed—but only by a man made unlike all other men" (208). With her heart burning for revenge, Amba arrived at a disreputable quarter for the transvestites in the backstreets of Bombay and underwent a painful operation to change her sex. The lissome fiancée of King Salva thus metamorphosed into Shikhandin, the mythological transvestite, and began to wait for her chance.

After the war it became clear that the independence of India was only a matter of time because the war-ravaged 'Britain no longer had the stomach for colonial conflict' (209). The Kaurava leaders were released from the prison to confront a completely changed political scenario: 'They discovered a nation whose nationalism had been left directionless too long, and a rival organization unrecognizably stronger than it had ever been developed while the Kauravas were atrophying in jail. Suddenly, the Independence stakes were a two-horse race, with the two horses aiming for different finishing posts' (210). In the ensuing elections to the provincial governments the Kaurava Party did well; it won the majority of the provinces. But Karna's Group captured most of the Muslim seats and demanded the partition of the country. The trial of the INA soldiers for treason at the Red Fort, which generated a tremendous upsurge of patriotism in the country, temporarily brought the rival parties closer: 'For the first time in their long careers Mohammed Ali Karna and Dhritarashtra accepted the same brief. The O O (Onward Organization) trials were the last issue on which the two parties took the same stand' (210). By the time the trial ended, it was obvious to everyone that the Labour Government in Britain was determined to dismantle their largest empire. Karna mounted immense pressure on the British to achieve his party's political aim—a separate land for the Muslims. When the British showed a hesitation to break the dominion they had so assiduously built over the century, the Muslim Group President urged his followers to resort to 'Direct Action' which led to an unprecedented communal flare-up in the subcontinent: 'Several thousand cadavers, burning vehicles, gutted homes, looted shops and rivulets of blood later, everyone except the Mahaguru began thinking about the unthinkable: the division of the motherland' (211).

The narrative takes note of Gangaji's slackening hold on the affairs of the state before Independence: 'Gangaji refused to be reconciled to the new reality. He walked in vain from riot-spot to riot-spot, trying to put out the conflagration through expressions of reason and grief' (211). But his old magic had vanished. His plea for unity was ignored by both the Kauravas and the Muslim Group. The nation—at least a greater part of it—disregarded the appeal of its father for non-violence, peace and amity. As the communal frenzy swept across the country, the British government appointed a new representative, Viscount Drewpad (Mountbatten), and sent him to India with the sole mandate to expedite and negotiate the transfer of power. Drewpad—the last viceroy of India—arrived in New Delhi with his charming wife, Georgina (Edwina), whom he would use as a 'secret weapon' (215) to dupe the Indian leaders, particularly the blind, and recently widowed, Dhritarashtra.

Book XI: *Renunciation—Or, The Bed of Arrows*

The first thing that the last British viceroy—'a superficial and supercilious man' (221), as Tharoor calls him—clarified to the Indian leaders was his government's determination to transfer power. It became unmistakably evident that the partition of the country was unavoidable. Gangaji's last attempt to preserve the integrity of the nation by suggesting that the Kauravas should accept Karna as the Prime Minister of united India was vetoed by Dhritarashtra. When the date was announced for the transfer of power (15 August 1947, which happened to be the wedding anniversary of Viscount Drewpad), Ganga Datta urged his followers not to give in to the demand for Partition. But his power-hungry heir-apparent ignored his plea: "Gangaji, we understand how you feel. . . . We have fought by your side for our freedom, all these years. We have imbibed your principles and convictions. You have led us to the brink of victory. . . . But now, the time has come for us to apply our principles in the face of the acid test of reality" (223). The party, which Ganga Datta had diligently built up and sacrificed his life for, thus went against him. Gangaji became irrelevant even before his death: 'That evening, the Working Committee of the Kaurava Party resolved unanimously to accept in principle the partition of the country. It was the first time we had ever gone against the expressed wishes of Gangaji. His era was over' (223).

Tharoor's version of India's struggle for freedom is unequivocally critical of Gandhi for loosening his control over the Congress Party at a time when it was needed most. Gandhi, in this postmodernist version, was mistaken in allowing the issue of partition to be decided by the leaders like Nehru who were no match for either Jinnah or Mountbatten. Justifying the Working Committee decision, which was later severely criticized as being taken in abnormal haste by leaders who—in their inordinate greed for power—sacrificed the unity of the country, Ved Vyas thus says: 'We gave in to Partition because Karna's inhuman obduracy and Drewpad's indecent haste left us no choice' (224). In hindsight he, however, admits that none of the Congress leaders was aware of the fact—highlighted by Dominique Lappierre and Larry Collins, among others—that Jinnah was seriously ill and he would die within a year of the country's partition. Nor could they foresee the magnitude of violence the vivisection of the country would result in. The haphazard manner in which the country was divided showed not only the indecent haste of the British to lay down their colonial burden and depart but also their absolute lack of respect for the people of the country they were about to leave. A political cartographer, Mr. Nichols (Cyril Radcliff) was appointed to hack the country on communal basis and award provinces to either India or Karnistan. The consequence of this arbitrary and thoughtless attempt to draw shadow lines across the subcontinent proved disastrous:

> Fat little Nichols drew his lines on his maps, and each stroke of his pencil generated other lines, less orderly and less erasable lines, lines of displaced human beings leading their families and animals away from the only homes they had ever known because they were suddenly to become foreigners there, lines of buses and bullock-carts and lorries and trains all laden with desperate humanity and their pathetic possessions, lines too of angry vicious predators with guns and knives flashing as they descended on the other lines, lines now of shooting hitting wounding raping killing looting attackers ripping apart the lines of stumbling fleeing bleeding crying screaming dying refugees. . . . In those days . . . lines meant lives. (225)

The Partition carnage, which led to the largest exodus in the history of mankind, was stunning in its magnitude and sheer mindlessness. Gangaji, who moved from one riot-torn area to another and prayed for peace and sanity, viewed the violence as a repudiation of his teaching and looked suddenly old. In utter despair perhaps, or due to senility, he started, at this stage, a strange and highly controversial experiment in self-restraint and self-perfection with his follower Sarah Moore: "She will lie with me, unclad, and cradle me in her arms, and I shall not be aroused. In that non-arousal I hope to satisfy myself that I have remained pure and disciplined" (228).

While the Mahaguru was seeking solace in the maternal arms of his Scottish disciple, his protégé—Dhritarashtra—developed a scandalous relationship with the British vicereine. Georgina Drewpad (Edwina Mountbatten), described as an 'amatory adventuress of libellous renown' (229), surrendered to the blind temptations of Dhritarashtra and, as the country was preparing to celebrate her emancipation from colonial rule, allowed the Prime Minister designate of the independent nation to take possession of her body. The narrator comments humorously, "No country whose colonists' imagination had created an Adela

Quested and a Daphne Manners could have denied its seed to the most yielding of its vicereines" (230). The novel implicates Nehru not only in the hasty deal of the partition of the country by colluding with Mountbatten and his seductive wife but also in developing an unholy liaison with the vicereine which was exploited by her wily husband for political purpose.

In the midst of Independence Day celebrations, when the Indian Tri-colour replaced the Union Jack and Dhritarashtra announced the country's historic tryst with destiny to the slumbering world, Gangaji—the most dejected man at the end of a prolonged struggle—fell victim to his assassin's bullets. Princess Amba, metamorphosed into Shikhandin (Nathuram Godse) confronted the celibate Father of the Nation and denounced him for dereliction of duty: "You make me sick, Bhishma. Your life has been a waste, unproductive, barren. You are nothing but an impotent old walrus sucking other reptiles' eggs, an infertile old fool . . . a man who is less than a woman. The tragedy of this country springs from you" (232). The invective sums up Ganga's/ Gandhi's life as a waste, a total failure. In order to reinforce the impact of the serious allegation, Tharoor deviates from the popularly known account of Gandhi's death and puts in the mouth of the dying leader not "Hey Ram" but "I . . . have . . . failed" (234).

Though the scene of Gandhi's death is transported to a mythic setting, the novelist quotes the actual words of many famous personalities like Einstein, Nehru, and Jinnah who spoke on the occasion. Ved Vyas's comment suggests a number of possible causes for Gandhi's death in which the people of the country were also implicated: "I will not ask whether Amba/ Shikhandin was truly responsible for the Mahaguru's death, or whether it was not India collectively that ended Gangaji's life by tearing itself apart. Nor will I ask . . . to reflect on whether Ganga Datta might in fact have been the victim of an overwhelming death-wish, a desire to end a life that he saw starkly as having served no purpose, a desire buried deep in the urge that had led him, all those years earlier, to create and nurture his own executioner" (234). The narrator does not categorically say whether he subscribes to the views of Gandhi's murderer but his overall tone suggests that the father of the nation died a defeated, desolate and disillusioned man.

Book XII: *The Man Who Could Not Be King*

If the history of pre-Independence India is dominated by Gandhi/ Ganga Datta, the narrative of the postcolonial era is overshadowed by blind Dhritarashtra (Nehru) and his arrogant daughter. While the former deals with the country's struggle against colonial rule under the leadership of Gangaji and his experiment with truth and non-violence which gave the nationalist movement an added significance, the latter examines the newly awakened nation's tryst with democracy under the stewardship of Ganga's chosen heir.

Tharoor's narrative details the immediate changes that followed the first flush of independence. The newspapers edited by Englishmen suddenly discovered great virtues in the national leaders whom they had reviled for years. The attitudinal shift was also reflected in the withdrawal of signs from exclusively European establishments which read: 'Indians and dogs not admitted.' Children endowed with magical powers were born at the midnight hour of Independence 'who would go on to label a generation and rejuvenate a literature' (240). British civil servants, who suddenly found themselves in urgent need to be obsequious and attentive to native Indians to whom they had condescended for centuries, began to apply for premature retirement and book their passages home. The change is demonstrated by the episode of Ronald Heaslop who begs favour from J.P. Drona, now a minister for Administrative Reform. Heaslop, who reappeared in Tharoor's novel from the pages of Forster's *A Passage to India* as a typical colonist, highly contemptuous of native Indians and their culture, is here shown as being paid in the same coin by nationalist Drona.

The most significant occurrence in those early years of Independence was the birth of D(raupadi) Mokrasi i.e. Democracy.

On 26 January 1950, when the newly drafted constitution of the Republic of India was promulgated by its founding fathers, Georgina Drewpad gave birth to a premature baby—the fruit of her illicit union with Dhritarashtra. The girl baby—having an indeterminate pink and brown complexion of her mixed parentage—was handed over to a low caste servant of the blind Prime Minister because 'neither of her parents could openly acknowledge the intimacy that had produced her' (244). Like Salman Rushdie, Tharoor thus debunks the established narrative of Indian history and repudiates the newly born democracy as an illegitimate product of the unholy liaison between Nehru and Edwina Mountbatten. Born at an inauspicious hour in a land 'racked with chaos and carnage' (245), the baby was named Draupadi by her adoptive parents and she grew up into a beautiful woman whose life gave meaning to the postcolonial story of the country.

The nation in those early years of freedom went through a continuous state of ferment. Everything in it was reshaped and reformed—its domestic and foreign policies, its official languages and politics, its internal organizations and international borders. The first major problem which confronted the new government was the future of the princely states. While most of these states decided to accede to either India or Karnistan 'according to the dictates of geography and common sense' (246), Manimir (Kashmir)—which was strategically located between the two nations—refused to do so and declared itself to be independent instead. Manimir was a Muslim dominated state ruled by a Hindu king, Maharaja Vyabhichar Singh (Hari Singh) who is presented in the novel as a perverted hedonist with 'a taste for Caucasian carnality' (246). The anxiety of Indian leaders to integrate the state is precisely explained by the narrator: 'The future of India as a secular nation depended on its ability to integrate a Muslim-majority state successfully, to nail Karna's lie that India's Muslims needed a country of their own in order to breathe free and flourish' (247). In the wake of a Karnistani invasion into the state, Vidur, now the Principal Secretary for Integration, air-dashed to Manimir's capital in the dead of night and persuaded the frolicking Maharaja to sign the Instrument of Accession.

The Indian army entered into the valley and pushed back the invaders with panache. But blind Dhritarashtra ordered a cease-fire at this opportune moment and bungled the whole issue by taking it—either on the advice of Mountbatten and his wife, as many people believe, or out of a sense of idealism, as others including the narrator suggest—to the United Nations. Thus Nehru's irrational decision and lack of foresight perpetually turned Kashmir into a disputed territory. As Ved Vyas laments, "So Manimir remained condemned to the label of 'disputed territory,' part of it in Karnistani hands, the bulk in ours. The state whose attachment to India was the most eloquent possible repudiation of the religious Partition paid a high price for Dhritarashtra's idealism" (260). The decision was openly criticized by both his government and party colleagues. But by that time the visionary Prime Minister had mastered the technique of 'political self-perpetuation' (261). He silenced all protests by issuing threats of resignation. It was, as the narrator observes, a technique which would be profoundly absorbed and perfected by Priya Duryodhani, the young Kaurava princess who grew up in the shadow of her widower father and was appointed his official hostess.

Meanwhile, Draupadi had survived 'the handicaps of her premature birth' (261) and improved her health. During Dhritarashtra's lifetime, her health remained stable because, despite his shortsightedness in many respects, her idealistic progenitor 'devoted a discreet eye and an equally discreet cheque book to her welfare' (261). With all her shortcomings, she became the centre of postcolonial politics in India and achieved the capacity to 'muddle through' (282), thus contradicting the colonial view of the country as (expressed in E.M. Forster's words) 'a muddle.'

Book XIII: *Passages through India*

As Draupadi grew up into a beautiful woman, the five Pandava brothers came out into the world with 'a rare heritage and an unusual education' (265). They resolved to follow their father, Pandu, and their teacher, Drona, into the political arena. With his idiosyncrasies and personal predilections, Drona could not stay long in the government. He resigned from Dhritarashtra's cabinet and went off to the countryside to devote himself to constructive work. In this philanthropic mission, he was accompanied by the five Pandavas and his own son, Ashwathaman. They undertook 'passages through India,' trying to raise the villagers' awareness of their democratic rights and helping the poor farmers to get their due from rich and exploitative landlords. They exposed the corruption as well as maladministration of the government and launched a crusade for land reform. Jayaprakash's biting criticism of Nehru's policy of rapid industrialization and urbanization at the cost of the landless poor and village people earned him the sobriquet 'saintly anarchist' and raised the hackles of the rulers.

Dhritarashtra became worried about the growing popularity of Jayaprakash and his followers, which he viewed as a political threat to his hitherto unchallenged authority, and sought his friend Konika (Krishna) Menon's advice. A noted socialist, Menon had spent the years of the freedom movement in London running the Indian Home Rule. After Independence, Dhritarashtra made him Indian High Commissioner to Great Britain. The witty and humorous exchange between the two friends evinces Tharoor's keen insight into Indian diplomacy. In a long incantatory verse, Konika gave the Prime Minister a Machiavellian counsel based on traditional treatise like Kautilya's *Arthashastra* and Vyasa's *Shantiparvan*: "Eradicate the slightest threat!/ Don't forget the thinnest thorn/ Embedded in your flesh, might yet/ Fester; and this I warn:/ A small spark can start a forest fire—/ No enemy's too minor—/ Before the danger gets too dire/ Don't make the fine points finer" (272). The verse suggests the elimination of political rivals to secure one's seat of power. Nehru, the true democrat, declined to follow Menon's advice ('that's simply not me, I can't do it,' he said) but his young daughter Duryodhani not only remembered every word of Menon's brutal counsel but also decided to act on it. 'She was glad,' Ved Vyas writes, 'her idealistic father had some less idealistic friends' (273).

Manipulation of power and suppression of dissent thus became the hallmarks of India's political culture after Independence. Priya Duryodhani's nefarious design to eliminate the Pandavas, who collectively represented the five pillars of Indian democracy, if succeeded, might have boosted her political ambition. But the timely intervention of Vidur (who, as the Secretary of the Home Ministry, remained above parochial and self-serving politics and served the nation with his sagacity and foresight) saved their lives. He intercepted the five brothers in their passage through the country, warned them of the impending danger, and sent them to the relative anonymity of Varanavata across the Ganges.

Meantime, Karna died after realizing his dream of establishing a country of the faithfuls named after him. When the news of the tragedy reached Dhritarashtra, he told Vidur that he had never liked the un-Islamic founder of the Islamic nation for his 'overweening ambition' (278). But he confessed: "if we had given [Karna] his due in the Kaurava Party, might he not today be remembered as one of the finest Indians of us all?" (278). And on hearing the news, Kunti—the widow of Pandu—wept silently for the son she had never known and 'shook her fist at the sun' (278).

Book XIV: *The Rigged Veda*

This chapter, like some others in the novel, makes room for a number of incidents from the epic which are not necessary for its historical narrative. These include Duryodhani's sinister plan to burn the Pandava brothers in the Lac House of Varanavata and Vidur's intervention to save their lives, their adventures during the years of exile, and Bhim's affair with Hidimba. But the incident of *Jatugriha* allegorically suggests Indira Gandhi's attempt to decimate her political opponents and undermine the democratic institutions of the country even before she came to power.

The defeat of Hidimba implies a parallel for the liberation of Goa from Portuguese rule while the Pandava's passage through India with their mother is used as an occasion to assess the state of affairs under Nehru's dispensation.

The idealistic Prime Minister ruled the country virtually unchallenged, with his daughter by his side. He inducted his friend Konika Menon into the cabinet as Minister of Defence and the two ivory tower politicians started implementing their unrealistic plans. The major Nehruvian policies become the target of the author's criticism in the novel. According to Tharoor, Nehru's excessive emphasis on heavy industries, which he called the 'new temples' of modern India, was ill-advised. Because it overlooked the unsavoury reality that nearly eighty percent of the country's population eked out a meagre existence without the basic amenities of life. It was also unfair and unwise to concentrate too much on establishing centres of higher learning because these institutions produced trained manpower for the international market and ignored the illiteracy of our own people. As the narrator says:

> Institutions of higher learning, colleges of technology, schools of management mushroomed in the dark humid forests of our ignorance. The British had neglected village education in their efforts to produce a limited literate class of petty clerks to turn the lower wheels of their bureaucracy, so we too neglected the villages in our efforts to widen that literate class for their new places at the top. Within a short while we would have the world's second largest pool of scientifically trained manpower, side by side with its largest lake of educated unemployed. Our medical schools produced the most gifted doctors in the hospitals of London, while whole districts ached without aspirin. Our institutes of technology were generously subsidized by our tax revenues to churn out brilliant graduates for the research laboratories of American corporations. (293-94)

The setting up of the centralised system of Parliamentary democracy during Nehru's tenure also proved inefficacious for a huge and diversified country like India because 'Parliament passed laws that a few implemented and many ignored' (293). Some of Tharoor's remarks about the country's first Prime Minister may sound harsh but in view of the paradigm shift in Indian economics in the early 1990s, which exposed the glaring limitations of the Nehruvian (and largely socialist) model of development and the inadequacy of the authority of the state to redress the country's socio-economic problems, the criticism appears largely justified.

The most serious complaint of the narrator against visionary Nehru is that he neglected the needs of the people at home and devoted his energies to gain international acclaim. Together with his ideological soul-mate Krishna Menon, Nehru evolved and promoted, during the Cold War, the concept of 'non-alignment' without assessing the strength of his own country to make the movement successful. In a bantering tone, Ved Vyas remarks that the socialist duo 'developed into a fine art the skill of speaking for the higher conscience of mankind' but none of them could 'control the convictions or even the conduct of those who were to implement their policies' (295).

The values represented by Dhritarashtra/ Nehru and Krishna Menon were far removed from the grass-root realities of India. In the narrator's opinion, the former was 'guilty . . . of the insincerity of the blind' while the latter of 'the inaccuracy of the ivory-tower' (295). This inevitably led them to display a desire for populism and bravado which was evinced by the military conquest and annexation of Comea (Goa). But the tediousness of uninterrupted and unchallenged rule (Nehru won handsomely in the three consecutive polls held since Independence) and the self-delusion of the visionary generated a sense of complacency. The disastrous consequences of this complacent and smug attitude of the rulers were borne out by the country's humiliating defeat at the hands of the Chinese in 1962. The fall-out of the military debacle was that under tremendous political pressure within and outside the Congress/ Kaurava Party, Krishna (Konika) Menon had to resign. And Nehru, the exponent of the policy of 'Panch Sil' and formulator of the slogan 'Hindi-Chini bhai bhai' was shocked by the Chinese perfidy. The failure of his much-flaunted foreign policy broke his heart and quickened his death.

Book XV: *The Act of Free Choice*

After Dhritarashtra's death, it became clear to all that India's first and longest serving Prime Minister had left no legacy for the democratic system of the country. As Draupadi Mokrasi's adoptive father said to the orphaned girl: "Dhritarashtra has left you nothing in his will" (309). For the first time since her birth, the girl found that she had to act out of free choice to decide her destiny and she resolutely announced: "I shall find my own husband" (310). She had grown into a beautiful woman. Despite her mixed origin, Indian democracy was of a darker hue and the very Indianness of her complexion made her all the more cherishable. Describing her intrinsic charm, Ved Vyas says, "she was warm. . . . Hers was not a beauty that held itself aloof; it was not arrogant, nor withdrawn, nor self-obsessed, indeed not even self-sufficient. . . . Draupadi's beauty was public, absorbing the beauty of the world around it, blossoming in the sunlight of popular adulation" (309).

In the aftermath of Dhritarashtra's death, the Kaurava Party found itself in the condition of a ship without a captain to steer it. The towering personality of Dhritarashtra had not allowed any leader to grow. There were a number of regional leaders who were very powerful in their respective provinces but none of them had the truly national stature to succeed the late Prime Minister. After prolonged deliberations, the Kaurava Working Committee decided that (a) the party would be run by collective leadership and (b) Shishu Pal (Lal Bahadur Shastri), who had an honest image but a limited influence, would be the country's new Premier. In the absence of a better alternative, the decision was accepted without protest, though there was doubt in the minds of many party workers about the efficiency of Shishu Pal to run the country. Nobody was sure that Indian democracy would not fall into wrong hands as it had fallen in the neighbouring Karnistan 'where a series of shambolic civilian administrations had been overthrown by a military coup' (310).

In order to dispel doubt and uncertainty from the minds of the party members, a special session was convened. It was in this camp that Draupadi met the Pandava brothers and bedazzled them with her scintillating beauty. It was here too that the power struggle began within the Kaurava organization, between Priya Duryodhani (Indira Gandhi) and the Pandavas who symbolized the five pillars of Indian democracy: Yudhishtir (Morarji Desai)—truth, righteousness and political wisdom; Bhim—the army; Arjun—the free press; Nakul and Sahadev—the administrative and the foreign services respectively. The hopes and limitations of the democratic institutions they served were embodied in them.

Notwithstanding envious Duryodhani's attempt to marry Draupadi off to Ekalavya, the low-caste pupil of socialist Drona who could be easily manipulated as a poverty-stricken philanderer, D. Mokrasi made her own choice. In a *swayamvara sabha*, presented by the narrator as a dream sequence, Arjun defeated a long line of eligible contenders in a battle of ballots and won the dark beauty. Allegorically, the union of Arjun, the embodiment of perfection, with Draupadi suggested the marriage of democracy with the voice of the people. But, by an ironic twist of events, she came to be shared equally by the five Pandava brothers because of the maternal injunction/advice of Kunti. Together they gave 'sustenance and protection' (321) to D(raupadi) Mokrasi who, in turn, ensured their unity.

Meanwhile, belying all misgivings, Shishu Pal proved himself to be a good Prime Minister in a 'decent and well-meaning way' (317). When the Karnistanis, who underestimated his strength, made a second attempt to capture Manimir, he taught the perfidious neighbours a lesson by inflicting on them a stunning defeat. But, unlike Dhritarashtra, Shishu Pal preferred peace to winning war and the 'preservation of life' (318) to taking revenge. He meticulously gave away every inch of the Karnistani territory which the Indian soldiers had won. But he died while signing the peace treaty at a conference table in Tashkent. The Kaurava Working Committee met once again and selected Priya Duryodhani as India's next Prime Minister because of her uncommon stature, deceptive docility and mistaken maneuverability. As Ved Vyas, the participant narrator, says, "We want a Prime Minister with certain limitations, a Prime Minister who is no more than any minister, a Prime Minister who will decorate the office . . . and let us run the country" (318).

While Dhritarashtra's daughter assumed office, the Pandava quintet—the collective husbands of D. Mokrasi—were sharing her through elaborate procedures and schedules. Arjun inadvertently violated one such rule and was banished for a year. He spent the period of exile travelling around the country as a roving journalist. Apart from enjoying the company of a succession of remarkable women like Ulupi and Chitrangada, he reported for a national newspaper some of the most sensational events of the time: the Naxalite movement in West Bengal, the Chipko movement in the foothills of the Himalayas, and the anti-Hindi agitation in Tamilnadu. At the end of his long passage through India, he arrived at an obscure southern town named Gokarnam and met the local M.L.A. and Secretary of the Kaurava Party, D. Krishna Parthasarathi, presented in the novel as a reduced and relegated figure of the mythological god in the *Mahabharata* who was the friend and charioteer of the prototype Arjun and the author of the *Gita.* It is noteworthy that a number of epic characters have been taken in the novel and assigned places in the twentieth century Indian politics. But the analogy often tends to be threadbare.

Tharoor's Krishna—a local politician and exponent of Ottamthullal dance—appears to be a pale latter-day shadow of the legendary god. Arjun spent the last part of his exile in Gokarnam as Krishna's guest and disciple. According to the narrator, the meeting between the two marked 'the beginning of a friendship that would transcend time, space and distance, and give meaning and purpose to Arjun's life' (328). But this is not sufficiently borne out by the text. Arjun falls in love with Krishna's sister

Subhadra and abducts her with his friend's help, after a farcical sexual escapade with a prostitute. Lacking ambition and satisfied with his life at Gokarnam, Krishna declined Arjun's invitation to join national politics but he agreed to give his brother-in-law as well as the nation his valuable advice in hours of need from a 'detached distance' (334). The episode detailing Arjun-Subhadra marriage and the birth of Abhimanyu, like the description of Krishna's superhuman attributes, does not fit in with the novel's historical narrative and seems to be extraneous to the needs of the story.

Book XVI: *The Bungle Book—Or, The Reign of Error*

After a year of Duryodhani's 'undistinguished and diffident' (339) rule, the country went to polls in the fourth general election after Independence. The Kaurava Party retained power at the centre but it lost seats all over India to a 'motley array of opposition groups' which cobbled together coalition governments in at least half-a-dozen states. The electoral setback widened the split in the Kaurava Party. In a post-election meeting of the Working Committee convened to take stock of the situation, the eldest Pandava, Yudhishtir, who had grown into a thin, bald, almost ascetic figure like Gangaji and begun to rival the latter's interest in fads, openly raised his voice of dissidence. He expressed serious doubt about the efficacy of Duryodhani's leadership to run the country: "If we had stronger leadership, this would not have happened" (339).

The bitter conflict between Duryodhani (Indira) and Yudhishtir (Morarji) over the responsibility of the electoral defeat and putting the Party in order was resolved with the Kaurava High Command arriving at a compromise: that there would be no change of leader, and that Yudhishtir would be made the Deputy Prime Minister. But the formula did not work for long. Duryodhani could not digest the humiliation of having her authority curtailed in this manner. She shook her earlier uncertainty and turned her diffidence into assertiveness. She became increasingly cold and distant in her behaviour with senior leaders of the Party and began to ignore the Deputy Prime Minister. She stopped sending him any file, refused to respond to his suggestions, and called cabinet meetings without bothering to intimate him. Insulted by the younger Prime Minister, Yudhishtir (Morarji) resigned from the cabinet.

While all this happened, D(raupadi) Mokrasi—long neglected by her guardians—fell seriously ill. With the intense fratricidal war within the ruling party, democracy suffered a setback and her condition deteriorated with every passing day. The resignation of Yudhishtir gave Duryodhani an opportunity to promote her own cause within the Party and the Government. She began to speak loudly about her father's socialist ideals which had been betrayed by what she termed 'the reactionary elements' within the Party. She appealed to all left, liberal and progressive forces outside the Kaurava organization to rally behind her effort to fulfil her father's socialist dream. One of the first to join her was Drona's son Ashwathaman (Chandrasekhar), who had inherited his socialist father's political mantle. Duryodhani used this Young Turk as a 'one-man ginger group' within the traditionalist party to push her populist agenda—like the abolition of privy purses and the nationalization of banks—to the detriment of the country's economy. On the issue of privy purse, she could enlist the support of the majority of the Kaurava Working Committee. But she failed to carry a majority of the party with her on the question of bank nationalization which the narrator sardonically describes as 'transferring functioning and successful institutions from the hands of competent capitalists to those of bumbling bureaucrats' (346).

Determined to foster her socialist credentials, Duryodhani called for a free vote in the Parliament and was able to pass the bill with the support of the leftist opposition parties. The legislative victory evinced Duryodhani's immense political clout at the cost of democratic process. But before the controversial bill was made into an Act with the Presidential signature, the scrupulous, decent and dignified figurehead of the nation, Dr Mehrban Imandar (Dr. Fakhruddin Ali Ahmed), passed away. The Presidential election gave the beleaguered and scattered Kaurava Old Guards an opportunity to regroup and teach Duryodhani, who had gone out of their control like 'Frankenstein's monster' (347), a lesson. With a view to reining in the recalcitrant Prime Minister and imposing a no-nonsense President on her, they chose Ved Vyas as the official candidate of the Party. But Duryodhani challenged the Party's decision by proposing the name of Ekalavya (V.V. Giri) as an independent candidate.

The election of the constitutional figurehead, the most acrimonious one in the country's postcolonial history which resulted in a narrow victory for Duryodhani's candidate, led to the split of 'the world's oldest anti-colonial political organization, sixteen years away from its centenary' (351). The majority went with Dhritarashtra's daughter and called themselves Kaurava (R) and the rest were dubbed Kaurava (O). For the first time since Independence, the Prime Minister did not enjoy the support of the majority in the Parliament. But her government survived with the support of the Left parties which were duped by her pseudo-egalitarianism and insincere socialist rhetoric.

After a year, during which the self-serving Prime Minister attacked 'big business and monopoly capital' (351) to win public support, Duryodhani called a snap poll. With a brilliantly coined campaign slogan 'Remove Poverty' she returned to power with a bigger parliamentary majority than even her illustrious father had ever enjoyed. Priya Duryodhani thus emerged victorious and 'stood alone amongst the ruins of her old party, having smashed to pieces all the pillars and foundations that had supported her in the past' (351). Instead of self-respecting Kauravas, she was now surrounded by shameless sycophants and supplicants 'prostrating themselves amidst the rubble' (351). After the amazing electoral victory, Duryodhani began to shine like an Empress and for a year or two she blinded the people with her brilliant new image. And all the while neglected D. Mokrasi suffered from one ailment or another.

The glorious moment in Duryodhani's political career was the Gelabi Desh (Bangladesh) War. Like Rushdie's *Midnight's*

Children, Tharoor's novel precisely analyses the reasons—political, cultural, linguistic et al—behind the revolt of the East Wing of Karnistan against the West and its declaration of independence. India intervened in the civil war of her neighbouring state because 'the repression of the Gelabins following the imposition of martial law sent a panic-stricken flood of brutalized humanity flooding across our borders to create, on Indian soil, the biggest refugee problem the world has ever known' (354).

Indian army liberated Gelabi Desh from Karnistani repression in, what the narrator describes as, 'one of only two wars in this century of carnage that can be morally justified' (355), and that lasted for seventeen days. The breaking up of Karnistan by Duryodhani is compared to the dismemberment of Jarasandha—the son of king Brihadratha—by Bhim in Vyasa's mythological narrative of the Rajasuya Yagna. The Gelabi Desh War, which deflated the myth of a nation held together by the glue of religion, invested Dhritarashtra's daughter with an aura of political invincibility: 'India accorded Duryodhani its ultimate accolade: she was not just deified, she was maternalized' (355).

But it did not take her long to dissipate her goodwill, her adulation and her enviable position in the hearts of the people. The mask of divinity was soon removed, revealing the unpalatable fact that 'she did not know what to do with any of it' (356). The political well-being of the Prime Minister was not converted into the well-being of the countrymen whose lives continued to be plagued by illiteracy, poverty and unemployment due to 'the heartless ineptness of the one in whom they had placed their trust' (356). It was a shameful betrayal of the people's trust by a bungling leader who was unresponsive to the call of duty. Duryodhani paid only lip service to the 'wretched of the Indian earth' (357) and began to accumulate more and more power in their name. The ugly symptoms of autocracy manifested themselves in her attempts to blackmail the press and create a 'committed' judiciary on the pretext of their being out of touch with the masses.

These whimsical attacks on the body politic generally weakened the democratic institutions in the country and this 'reign of error' paved the way for a rule of terror: "while the poor remained as poor as they had ever been, while striking trade unionists were beaten and arrested, while peasant demonstrations were assaulted and broken . . . more and more laws went on to the statute books empowering Priya Duryodhani to prohibit, proscribe, profane, prolate, prosecute or prostitute all the freedoms the national movement had fought to attain" (357). This autocratic rule, which would culminate in the midnight declaration of the Emergency and suspension of civil rights, is symbolically presented through the mythological story of a conflagration ignited by Agni, the god of fire, which consumed a huge forest and completely devastated its flora and fauna.

Book XVII: *The Drop of Honey—A Parable*

The inevitable result of Duryodhani's autocratic rule, which turned her into a menacingly arrogant person and threatened the very foundation of the country's democratic structure, was a popular uprising against her led by Jayaprakash Drona. The dishonesty and cynicism of the corrupt government affronted the conscience of the freedom fighter and he openly called for a restoration of India's ancient values to the country's governance. The uprising fired the people's imagination and was transformed into a mass movement in which the opposition parties could not help but join. Drona lashed out not only against Dhritarashtra's daughter but against all the evils she had failed to eradicate and 'therefore . . . had herself come to represent: venality and corruption, police brutality and bureaucratic inefficiency, rising prices . . . and black-marketing' (363). She was held responsible for the betrayal of the people's hopes and expectations. Duryodhani (Indira Gandhi) thus paid the price for her complete identification with her party and the nation through a sycophantic and fascist slogan ('Indira is India'). The Jayaprakash-led movement rocked the central government and made it unstable. The Kaurava (R)-ruled state governments, run by Duryodhani's handpicked minions, who became notorious for their ineptitude and servility, were also completely paralysed. The political tide seemed to turn away from the country's Prime Minister to the hands of her opponents.

It is interesting to note that Tharoor's interpretation of the political situation in the country prior to the declaration of the Emergency is strikingly different from that of other writers like Rushdie who wrote about this period. Tharoor is critical of Indira Gandhi but he holds Jayaprakash Narayan and the assorted opposition for the political chaos in the country: "I was no admirer of Priya Duryodhani or what she stood for, but I was equally distraught about Drona's Popular Uprising and where it was leading the government" (364). He thinks that the opposition could have waited for the next election, which was not far away, and voted Indira out of power. Instead they chose a political short-cut and clamoured for her removal, that too not in the Parliament, where they had been reduced to a ridiculous minority, but in the street. In his view, the opposition parties cornered Indira and forced her to fight back: 'Priya Duryodhani had her back to the wall, and that was the position from which she always fought the hardest' (364).

The political crisis was intensified by a verdict of the Allahabad High Court which found Duryodhani guilty of electoral malpractice (sharing a platform with the President, a non-political figure-head, during her election campaign) and 'deprived her of her parliamentary privileges pending appeal' (365). Emboldened by the court verdict, the Popular Uprising demanded her resignation. But the beleaguered Prime Minister fought back by declaring an internal Siege on the advice of her closest advisor and hand-picked President of Kaurava (R), Shakuni Shankar Dey (Siddhartha Shankar Roy). The decision to impose Siege on the ground of a 'grave threat to the stability and security of the nation from internal disruption' (366), which was endorsed by the obliging President, Ekalavya, proved to be the most disastrous part of Duryodhani's political career. In the name of securing the country's stability, a state of anarchy was let loose. Midnight arrests of Opposition and Trade Union leaders were followed by Press censorship, suspension of fundamental rights and adopting 'measures to put the judiciary in their place' (366). But these draconian measures to suppress opposition only served to unite the diverse constituents of the People's Uprising in a loose—and purely expedient—coalition called 'Janata Morcha" or 'People's Front.'

Significantly, Tharoor's assessment of the Emergency is markedly different from that of Rushdie. While in *Midnight's Children* the two-year-long despotic regime of Indira Gandhi, metaphorically described as an endless midnight, becomes the focal point of degeneration in the country's secular polity and democratic set-up, in *The Great Indian Novel* it appears to be only a part of the deteriorating political culture of India since independence. As a result, the blame on Indira Priyadarshini, who tolled the knell of democracy in the country through the proclamation of the Siege, is not as pronounced as it is in Rushdie's book which described the widowed Prime Minister as a 'Black Widow' castrating the people of the nation with the help of her sinister minions.

Tharoor does not join 'the chorus of condemnation' which was raised in the Western press about what had exactly happened during those months of the country's brush with dictatorship. He is doubtlessly critical of Indira's decision, which he terms 'cynical' and 'self-serving' but, at the same time, blames people like Jayaprakash Narayan (Drona) who compelled her to take this extreme step: "I still believed that the political chaos in the country, fuelled by Drona's idealistic but confused Uprising which a variety of political opportunists had joined and exploited, could have led the country nowhere but to anarchy" (369). In Tharoor's view, the Emergency was not uniformly evil. The implementation of a twenty-point socio-economic programme for the common people and the banning of political demonstrations and strike gave the nation a sense of purpose and direction which replaced the earlier drift and uncertainty. The narrator thus says, "I felt . . . that if the Siege, however base its motive, was going to permit the government to serve the common man far more effectively than before, then people like us, who had lost the freedoms we alone knew how to exercise, had no right to object" (369).

The Emergency also gives the narrator an occasion for making some perceptive comments on the Indian character and the institutional structure of the nation's polity. His conversation with Arjun at the height of Duryodhani's repressive rule contains a trenchant critique of the prevailing system of parliamentary democracy and the governmental process in the country which have always ignored the vast masses of people and their needs. Ved Vyas tells Arjun that Indians have, from the days of Nehru, only respected facades of parliamentary democracy but ignored their substance: "We ignored the basic fact that parliamentary democracy can only work if those who run it are constantly responsive to the needs of the people, and if the parliamentarians are qualified to legislate. Neither condition was fulfilled in India for long" (371).

He makes an even more cutting remark about the character of Indian people through the Puranic parable of 'the drop of honey' which 'illustrates both our resilience and our self-absorption in the face of circumstance' (371). The marvellous parable explains the secret of the Indians' capacity for survival in the face of odds: "One strength of the Indian mind is that it knows some problems cannot be resolved, and it learns to make the best of them. That is the Indian answer to the insuperable difficulty. . . . This is our national aesthetic. Without it, Arjun, India as we know it could not survive" (372). In a cynical tone, the narrator observes that Duryodhani's Siege did not really deserve to be condemned because the democratic process in the country had been atrophied and the ordinary mass of people had been divorced from it: "It was . . . a typical case of mind over matter—if you don't mind, it doesn't matter" (374). But Arjun rejected the depressing cynicism of the narrator and told him with greater conviction: "You've got to be wrong, or the whole world wouldn't make sense any more" (374).

The gentle but emphatic words of Arjun shattered the narrator's mental equipoise and compelled him to notice, without any ambivalence, the real condition of Draupadi during Duryodhani's authoritarian rule: "Can I admit the terrible suspicion that her own husbands were ill-treating her, exploiting her, neglecting her, even ignoring her, and still excuse myself for having done nothing about it?" (374). The sorry state of democracy in the country smashed his complacency and, being unable to confront the grim reality, he began to dream.

A remarkable stylistic feature of Tharoor's novel is that in order to solve the problem of fitting some important incidents from the epic into the chronological frame of the historical narrative, the author shifts them to a dream world where characters from contemporary history are "transported incongruously through time to their oneiric mythological settings" (355). The infamous game of dice between Yudhishtir and Shakuni in the court of Dhritarashtra and the consequent disrobing of Draupadi by Duryodhani's henchmen is an example of Tharoor's creative use of the mythic setting. The episode is used as a symbolic parallel for denuding Indian people of their dignity, freedom and democratic rights by Nehru's daughter and her handpicked minions during the Emergency. The intervention of Krishna in response to Draupadi's prayer to save her honour contains a stern warning for all future tyrants: "'However hard you try, Priya Duryodhani,' he said in a calm, deep voice, 'you and your men will never succeed in stripping Draupadi Mokrasi completely. In our country, she will always have enough to maintain her self-respect. But what about yours?'" (382).

When Ved Vyas woke up from his dream, he found that his earlier ambivalence was gone. He was now convinced of the evil intent of the Siege and he realized that Duryodhani and her shameless cohorts had been trying to strip the nation of the values which the people had earned through great sacrifice. Looking around him, he found that the reasons for which he had so far suspended his criticism of the Siege were not tenable: "The poor were not getting a better deal as a result of the suspension of the freedoms of the relatively privileged; if anything, they were worse off than before" (384). The suspension of freedoms and the abrogation of constitutional rights created a stifling atmosphere which permitted no outlet for the people's frustration. The ineffable plight of the nation led Krishna to end his self-imposed detachment from national politics and rise against the tyranny of Priya Duryodhani. His decisive action converted the irresolute Arjun and inspired him to rescue the people from the autocracy of an arrogant Prime Minister.

Book XVIII: *The Path to Salvation*

At the height of the repressive rule, Priya Duryodhani surprised the world by quite inexplicably withdrawing the Siege and announcing a general election. Several theories were advanced by political analysts to explain her sudden change of heart. Some people suggested that the Prime Minister had taken the risk at the advice of her favourite astrologer while others held the view that she had suspended the Siege to outrival her Karnistani counterpart Zaleel Shah Jhoota (Zulfikar Ali Bhutto) who had also called for elections in his country to earn international credit for the show of democracy. Still others thought that Dhritarashtra's daughter had decided to face the electorate at the suggestions of her intelligence agencies.

Whatever the reasons might be, the election gave the Indian voters a rare chance to choose between democracy and dictatorship and, for some people even, between dharma and adharma. The historic battle of ballots for the restoration of democracy and dharma revived the memory of the epic battle of Kurukshetra. The narrator, however, finds such comparison superficial. "The story of the *Mahabharata*," he says, "does not end on the field of battle. What happens afterwards is tragedy, suffering, futility, death. This underlines the only moral of that battle, and that epic: that there are no real victors. Everyone loses at the end" (391). Instead, he found in this electoral battle of the Indian people to regain their lost freedom a similarity with the historic freedom struggle: "I saw the great cause of Gangaji and Dhritarashtra and

Pandu thrillingly reborn in the hearts and minds of young crowds. . . . I saw the meaning of Independence come pulsating to life as unlettered peasants rose in the villages to pledge their votes for democracy" (392).

Indeed, the issue over which that particular election was fought was an unusual one: 'the rout or the restoration of democracy.' For the first time in his political career, Krishna took a keen interest in national politics. Both the contending parties—Kaurava (R) and the combined opposition—came to seek his help. He gave his experienced cadres to fight for Duryodhani's Kaurava Party while he himself 'went on to animate the opposition's national campaign' (393). Krishna's most difficult task was to persuade Arjun, who was assailed by doubts and misgivings at the moment of filing his nomination papers: "Is it right—should I fight—or if I just write, won't I cast more light?" (393).

In a long philosophical discourse, which is reminiscent of the famous dialogue between despondent Arjun and his omniscient charioteer before the epic battle of Kurukshetra, Krishna enjoined his brother-in-law to make up his mind and fight for the restoration of freedom: "If you don't fight now, you won't have anything to write about afterwards" (393). His *Gita* is modelled not on the original but on Vikram Seth's *The Golden Gate*. Like Seth's verse novel, it combines the serious and the profane and is parodic in nature:

> In other words, Arjun, don't waver,
> It's unworthy to neglect your duty
> Duryodhani is the country's enslaver:
> She's no village belle or city cutie.
> You must take a grip on yourself,
> Not flap like a maid on the shelf. (395)

At the end of this long sermon delivered in iambic tetrameter, Arjun's doubts were dispelled. He was convinced of the indestructibility of human spirit, as of the evil nature of Duryodhani's rule, and resolved to take active part in the decisive battle for democracy:

'You're right,' he said, 'Thanks, dear Krishna!
For playing vicar to my weak parishioner.
I was silly to be so irresolute.
Instead of thinking of the Spirit
And acting without heed to merit,
I'd wept and whined like a broken flute.
That's all over now! I'm ready to act—
Let's get the Opposition into an electoral pact!' (398)

The People's Front was soon joined by the deserters of Duryodhani's camp as well as her erstwhile supporters like Ashwathaman who had been ill-treated and imprisoned during the Siege. The battle-lines were clearly drawn and the campaign raged intensely. The bureaucracy and the army abstained, on Krishna's request, from the historic battle in which every one took sides. The Front cashed in on the people's wrath against Duryodhani and was overwhelmingly voted to power.

In order to avoid a contest among the constituents of the coalition, Drona—its architect and political mentor—and Ved Vyas—the eldest member of the Kaurava (O)—took upon themselves the responsibility of designating the new Prime Minister. After examining all the alternatives, they declared Yudhishtir (Morarji Desai) as the country's new leader for his unquestionable honesty and seniority. In retrospect, however, Ved Vyas understood 'the irony of beginning the era of the restoration of democracy with so undemocratic a procedure' (403). Tharoor's skepticism about the worthiness of the politicians who defeated Priya Duryodhani and came to power is revealed in a scathing remark: 'The Indian people gave themselves the privilege of replacing a determined, collected tyrant with an indeterminate collection of tyros' (402).

The euphoria of the Front's victory and the hopes raised by the new government did not last long. These were betrayed by the 'mutual competition and recrimination' (404) among the leaders of the coalition government which soon dissipated its energy. The humourless and self-righteous leader of the Front failed to keep his motley crew together and embarrassed the nation by openly advertising his personal fad: 'As the Prime Minister unsmilingly continued to make himself the laughing-stock of the nation, his coalition gradually unravelled beneath his feet. Write it on his epitaph, Ganapathi: our Hero piddled while home burned' (405). As a result, lawlessness broke out, prices skyrocketed, and government offices stopped functioning as 'every policy decision was hamstrung by factional disagreement' (405).

Within months of assuming office, the Janata Front government was turned into a 'vehicle for the personal ambitions of at least three veteran politicians besides the Prime Minister' (405). The three veterans were the self-styled champions of the backward strata of Indian society, namely Chowdhury Charan Singh, Jagjivan Ram and Raj Narain. The only issue over which the feuding factions agreed was the trial of Duryodhani on the charge of the subversion of the constitution. But the trial, conducted by a commission, proved to be abortive as the lawyers of the former Prime Minister dragged it on and on until the bored nation almost forgot it.

The crisis within the People's Front came to a head over a trivial issue—the government's attitude towards the untouchables—and its fragile unity crumbled with the withdrawal of support by the disgruntled legislators and leaders including Ashwathaman, the ruling coalition's radical President. They joined the shrill chorus of Priya Duryodhani denouncing the Yudhishtir government for its casteist bias. Jayaprakash Drona, the new 'messiah' of the nation, was disappointed at this unfortunate turn of events which shattered his dream of restoring the country's ancient glory and traditional values. Torn between his divided loyalty to the Front government he had brought into being and to his son who had changed the course of his life years ago, he fell sick. In order to muster support for his leadership and save his government, the self-righteous Yudhishtir, who had never told a lie in his life, took recourse to a deception. He fabricated a lie about Ashwathaman's death in an accident, which broke Drona's heart, and unscrupulously used the dying leader's plea for unity. Jayaprakash Drona (Narayan) died a sad, lonely and disappointed man.

In a glowing tribute to this untainted and saintly leader, the narrator compares him with Gangaji and gives him credit for raising the consciousness of the people about their rights and providing constructive support to the pillars of Indian democracy. At the same time he holds Drona indirectly responsible for the untimely demise of the People's Front: 'Drona's abhorrence of power had made him unfit to wield it. He had offered inspiration but not involvement, charisma but not change, hope but no harness. Having abandoned politics . . . he tried to stay above it all after the fall of Dhritarashtra's daughter, and so he let the revolution he had wrought fall into the hands of lesser men who were unworthy of his ideals' (409).

Yudhishtir's deception failed to save the government. It fell and in the election that followed Priya Duryodhani returned to power riding a wave of popular disenchantment with the Janata Front misrule.

The Great Indian Novel, thus, becomes a severe indictment of Indian politics since independence. It is a story of 'betrayed expectations' (411) and disappointed hopes enkindled by the country's emancipation from colonial rule. The narrative, which depicts the nation's political vicissitudes before and after its historic 'tryst with destiny,' conveys the author's sense of disappointment with its declining values and culture. According to Tharoor, the general politics of the country and her democratic institutions have deplorably failed to uphold her ancient values and traditions and bring about any remarkable change which was visualized by the freedom fighters. The narrator finds an all-pervasive degradation in national life: 'How far we have travelled from the glory and splendour of our adventurous mythological heroes! The land of Rama . . . the land where truth and honour and valour and dharma were worshipped as the cardinal principles of existence, is now a nation of weak-willed compromisers, of leaders unable to lead, of rampant corruption and endemic faithlessness" (411).

The narrative shows how far post-independence India has travelled from the 'India of the epic warriors [who] died on its mythological battlefields' and 'where epic battles [were] fought for great causes' (412). In India today mediocrity reigns and moneymaking is the greatest cause. Here power has become an end in itself rather than a means for effecting social change and the real political issues involve not any principles but parochialism. The country has been turned into a 'muddle' by her self-seeking and power-crazy politicians—the modern prototypes of the ancient Kauravas, who wrecked the glorious heritage of India represented by Bhishma in the *Mahabharata* and Gandhi in the recent past. The narrator envisions a bleak future for the country and seeks to escape from this chaos-ridden land into a world of dream because he feels that the process of devastation overtaking the country is irreversible. The concluding part of the novel describing the ascent of Yudhishtir to heaven ('The Path to Salvation'), which has no parallel in contemporary history, is thus presented as a dream-sequence. The scene is reproduced as it was in the epic except for the final argument of Yudhishtir with the god called Dharma over the interpretation of the concept known as *dharma*. The god of justice and righteousness, who puts the eldest Pandava through a series of difficult tests before granting him a vision of Paradise, speaks of the need and importance of practising *dharma* which alone can steer a people through the vicissitudes of history. Yudhishtir's true father says to him, "If there is one great Indian principle that has been handed down through the ages, it is that of the paramount importance of practising dharma at any price. Life itself is worthless without dharma. Only dharma is eternal" (417). But Yudhishtir refuses to be convinced by Dharma's assertion. He points out that the dharma appropriate for the country has varied at different stages of its evolution. Consequently, no single interpretation of the term, which is valid and relevant for all the ages, is possible.

Revealing a postmodernist sensibility, Tharoor's Yudhishtir stresses the necessity of accepting doubt and diversity as well as multiple interpretations of *dharma*, since he believes that 'there are no classical verities valid for all time' (418). It is the insistence on a unitary and dogmatic interpretation of dharma which has led to conflict in the life of the nation in the past as well as in the present. The country can find liberation from the bondage of history, which farcically repeats its mistakes, only by allowing or accepting diversity. He, therefore, proclaims emphatically: "Admit that there is more than one Truth, more than one Right, more than one dharma" (418). Yudhishtir's assertion of the multiplicity of truth and *dharma* seems to contain the political message of the novel. The book ends on a note of uncertainty with Ved Vyas waking up from his uneasy dream to an India 'muddling chaotically through to the twenty-first century' (418), and resolving to rewrite his story from a different perspective which would work out in fictional terms Yudhishtir's suggestions. Thus, there is a circularity about the narrative; it ends with a fresh beginning, the concluding line of the novel being the same as its opening line.

Adjuncts of History: A Study of Shashi Tharoor's *The Great Indian Novel*

SUDHENDU SHEKHAR
Government College, Panchmarhi

Like Salman Rushdie's *Midnight's Children*, Shashi Tharoor's *The Great Indian Novel* (1989) has been inspired by a sense of urgency and outrage on account of general erosion of values and norms in the post-Partition Indian polity. The author seems to have been most upset by the darkest period in the history of free India, i.e. the Emergency promulgated in 1975, and conceptualizes that experience into an existential riddle to be solved through the understanding of a parallel happening in the remote Indian past. Where Rushdie examines the psyche of his characters *suo moto*, Tharoor does so *sui generis*. Even as Rushdie's *Midnight's Children* corresponds to Tharoor's *The Great Indian Novel* thematically, they differ in their narratological intents.

The difference, through which Tharoor carves out a niche for himself, is the replacement of a piecemeal, convenient, multiform structure of fantasy by an elaborate, integrated corpus of myth. Undoubtedly, both apply subversive to the existing order of reality. Tharoor, however, schematically revives a vital chord in the common consciousness, and anticipates the direction of events with respect to that. It is this reawakening of the common consciousness that is significant in the entire construct of his craft, because of which Tharoor's history becomes a transcendental vision of the past, and an added facility to the understanding of the past by capitalizing on inherent cultural resources. It is within the ambit of this common cultural consciousness that the novelist uses myth. He does not scan history intuitively, but enlightened with available cultural motif.

In its historical content, myths have long been part of orally transmitted tradition, permeating the common cultural heritage. They occur as values of deep adherence, relating to the continuous universal identity of man. Even as man evolves, he retains the features of identity reflected in the cultural moorings of the past. He tries to come to terms with his present retrospectively, and overgrown with hindsight. Clearly, it is this perception of identity, which endows the readers of *The Great Indian Novel* with the cognitive flexibility only assiduously to be found in Rushdie's fiction. Rushdie's use of myth is sparing, referential, and context-bound, but Tharoor's is cognate, correlative and content-bound. If Rushdie enjoys all the liberties that postmodernism allows to penetrate into the object of deconstruction, Tharoor opts for a more restrained, congenial but essential way of doing so. In their respective treatments of history, Rushdie tries to effect his identity whereas Tharoor aims at reviving it. Indian mythology, in its stupendous diversity, provides many motifs to correlate various aspects of human life.

Like the *Ramayana*, the *Mahabharata* is a unitary national myth that perceives human life in totality, and supplies for Tharoor's novel the most appropriate allegorical background to project the contemporary Indian situation. He uses the mythic setting of the ancient epic to foreground the eternal present, the continuance of the historical process from India's remote past to the present. It operates in the manner of Rushdie's fantasy, which corresponds to the reality only obliquely, howsoever deliberate the desire of questioning the present may be. But it is not a case of mythography as history, which J.S. Negi understands thus: "Myths might have originated in chronological sequence but the manner in which they have been recorded all over the world hardly admits of temporal classification. Similarly their defusive character makes them overflow the confines of space. Mythography is therefore not the same as historiography of myths. They can only be studied in terms of their themes and forms, i.e. motifs."[1]

Finding correlation between myth and reality is a characteristic habit of the human mind, particularly in a civilization as old as the Indian. It is acutely conscious of the recurrence of mythic patterns and meanings in the contemporary events. Mythic and legendary characters are inseparable contemporaries for Indians who perpetually identify with the motifs of the two great epics—the *Ramayana* and the *Mahabharata*. In Rushdie's phrase, the people of this "myth-ridden land," conjure up patterns of similarity in the interwoven private and public lives with what remains ever alive in their memory.

Tharoor's facility in the identification of values is due to this structure of common experience. While subverting and sustaining the setting, psyche and identity of the past for the regeneration of the present, he brings in his ethnic consciousness into play, and is certainly more poised and pragmatic than the ceaseless experimenter in Rushdie. The cultural renaissance Tharoor envisages is premised on common memory and handy correlation, or a fictional order that is fewer contingents upon imagination. In fact, the life present is spontaneously stylized as the story memorized. As Paul Ricoeur observes: "Stories are recounted and not lived; life is lived and not recounted. . . . An unbridgeable gap seems to separate fiction and life. . . . If it is true that fiction is only completed in life and that life can be understood only through the stories we tell about it, then an examined life in the sense of the word as we have borrowed from Socrates, is a life recounted."[2]

The Great Indian Novel is the *Mahabharata* recounted because Tharoor does not fashion life, independent of the past patterns, and uses myth elaborately to function as the prototype. In a marked improvement upon Rushdie's craft, he sustains the endemic habitual past through the reciprocal present unlike what Rushdie and other suppose *ab initio* or the here-and-now perceived. This indulgent use of myth only naturally releases us from the continuum of the present for introspection and evaluation.

Apart from myth, which is part of the narrative aesthetics of Tharoor's novel and provides the value-structure to refer to, it is contemporary history that effects the domain of experience or the perceptional state. Embodied in the past, the characters feel and act in the present. There is no deliberate or overt overlapping of the past into the present. The novelist works as impressionist in contriving the continuing mental associations as catalyst for monitoring the system of history. What is borne out by individual entity and perception in Rusdhie's fiction is paradigmatically presented as individual creed and calling by Tharoor. A particular type is pitted against a new set of historical imperatives. Instead of casting a host of individual characters to fabricate a definitive existential situation in a piecemeal way, he devises the entire mythical structure, introducing the technique of ellipsis or condensation. To encompass the complexity of existence, he brings in what Kundera thinks is the Czech composer, Leos Janacek's (1854-1928) way of composition: "Roughly the same idea applies to the novel: it too is weighed down by 'technique,' by the conventions—that do the author's work for him: present a character, describe a milieu, bring the action into a historical situation, fill time in the character's lives with superfluous episodes, each shift of scene calls for a new exposition, description, explanation. My own imperative is 'Janacekian': to rid the novel of the automation of novelistic technique, of novelistic verbalism; to make it dense."[3]

The mythical structure of *The Great Indian Novel* also underlines the continuance of the historical process, the pastness of the present and the presentness of the past. Echoing T.S. Eliot's concept of time, the novelist conceives of simultaneous existence and order with the mythical characters and setting. Examining the process of meaning in myth, we get a structure, which, as a system of symbols, possesses a reality, independent of concept. In fact, while tracing the origin of this process we come to the understanding of the structure as a springboard for ideas. We think over the patterns and values of life, and relate them to the politico-cultural ethos of our own time. Or otherwise, it only expresses fears of repetitions of the event, and limitations of the individual. Says Lillian Feder: "Myth is a narrative structure of two basic areas of unconscious experience, which are, of course, related. First, it expresses instinctual drives and the repressed wishes, fears and conflicts that they motivate. Second, myth also conveys the remnants within the individual consciousness of the early stage of the phylogenetic development in which myths were created. This characteristic is evident mainly in its plots. Myth is a story involving human limitation and superhuman strivings and accomplishments which suggests through action usually of a ritual, ceremonial, or compulsive nature—man's attempt to express and thus control his own anxiety about those features of his physiological and psychological make-up and his external environment, which he cannot comprehend, accept or master."[4]

Clearly, to avert the modern editions of the Kurukshetra such as the Emergency of 1975, the novelist is concerned and protective about values that can obviate the follow-up to the climactic event. Preservation of values is, according to him, to uphold *dharma*, which is, in Betty Heimann's version, "a total cosmic responsibility, including God's, a universal justice far more inclusive, wider and profounder than any Western equivalent, such as 'duty.'"[5]

The motivated, selective enforcement of *dharma* brings, in the long run, a trail of miseries, and disorganization of priorities in the system as is apparent from the *Mahabharata*. This myth, therefore, not only serves to highlight the moral, ethical pitfalls but also provokes thinking on that score to redeem and refashion values of universal human importance in our progressive existence. As the narrator-protagonist of the novel, Ved Vyas, sums up,

> History is Kurukshetra. The struggle between *dharma* and *adharma* is a struggle of our nation, and each one of us in it, engages in on every single day of our existence. (391)

To 'counter the crushing burden of tradition and history,' Shashi Tharoor's protagonist uses his mythological connection as adjuncts of the study of present political evolution. Tharoor attempts to inspire a different politico-cultural consciousness, which may help transcend the limitations and absurdities of the human roles in the past socio-political set-up. His protagonist is keen on revising his story, which, he feels, has been told 'from a completely mistaken perspective.' (418) This 'mistrust of interpreting the past'[6] stems from the need of appropriating the present from a new perspective, accommodating a plurality of perceptions.

II

Divided into eighteen books on the pattern of the great epic, *The Great Indian Novel* takes on the entire subcontinent beginning with India under the British in the late nineteenth/early twentieth century down to India in the post-Emergency period. It covers all the major political historical events of the twentieth century—the events of national freedom movement like the Champaran Satyagrah, the Dandi March, the Round Table Conference and the Quit India Movement along with the events of the Partition, India's Independence, the wars with China and Pakistan, the liberation of Goa, the Emergency and after.

Writing about *The Great Indian Novel*, Shashi Tharoor sets out his intention: "*The Great Indian Novel* speaks for an India of multiple realities and multiple interpretation of reality. Throughout the novel runs an acknowledgement of the multiplicity of truth that has given shape and substance to the idea of India."[7] But these realities about India conveniently fall into the categories of good and bad, transitory and lasting, wishful and undesirable. The India Tharoor talks of is as much a product of virtues as vices, and demonstrates in their consummation a purpose of enlightenment, and awareness of the pitfalls that could have been avoided to pre-empt the process of the big events like the Partition and the Emergency. India, as of now, emerged in the freedom struggle, when various strands of social, political and cultural consciousness converged. It was a heroic mass struggle against an alien power structure, which subjugated India on the plea of trade. As this common colonial enemy is defeated, and the power is to be inherited, shared and administered, enemy from within disrupts and divides. This strange reality unfolding the inner self of man, imparts a value or creed to every calling, which culminates in the realization of a momentary identity rather than the eternal. The process of being together is forgotten for the products of self-serving ends. The fight between the personal and the permanent or larger value of human existence is ever-going, and the need to suppose and sustain how best the worst could be avoided is somewhat basic in the history of mankind as underscored here.

"Many of the characters, incidents and issues in this novel are based on," states Tharoor in the 'Afterword,' "the people and events described in great epic the *Mahabharata*, a work which remains a perennial source of delight and inspiration to millions in India." What operates as the genesis of this scheme is the idea that the battle of Kurukshetra is never over. However, Kurukshetra is also the occasion for rehabilitating values, and upholding *dharma*, which is always at stake, owing to myopic perception of the reality of the self and time. When the eternal reality of oneness and being ever-present is segregated into multiple manifestations of power, the conflict arises. The really powerful subsumes those realities, and becomes larger than the multiple selves:

> The self that means the object is identical with the larger self that possesses the object, just as when you seek the lost idea you are already in essence with the self that possesses the lost idea.[8]

The question of sharing the kingdom of Hastinapur not only pitted the Pandavas and the Kauravas against each other but also led to the battle of Kurukshetra. Likewise, the question of sharing power in free India decided the course of history after 1947, and ultimately led to the clamping of the Emergency. Once it was the values of Bhishma which were put paid to, and, on the other hand, those of Mahatma Gandhi in the recent past. The simple plot of values of collective experience being deserted for individual benefit of tasting the fruits of power and the consequent chaos informs the text of the *Mahabharata* as well as of *The Great Indian Novel*.

Chaos is the conspicuous theme of *The Great Indian Novel*. The political history of modern India, bearing resemblance to the events and the characters of a bygone period, underlines the evolution of chaos as a result of the foibles and follies of the political personalities with responsibility. They fail to live up to their expectations and equate that responsibility community-wise, instead indulge in self-aggrandizement. The upholders of *dharma* in the two texts—Bhishma and Gandhi—fell sacrificial victims to their own progenies and proteges, for their inability to reconcile the imperatives of power. The vows of celibacy and loyalty to the throne of Hastinapur on the part of Bhishma, and those of commitment to the path of truth and non-violence for attaining and maintaining independence for India on the part of Mahatma Gandhi respectively turned out to be their traps of existence, virtually undoing all they had stood for.

The self-styled heirs to the throne of the Kingdom and that of the nation could not bring their respective vision and spirit to the seat of power, or otherwise they could not accommodate the multiplicity of their challenges to the administration of their constituency. The intellectual naivete, and complacent self-righteousness they exemplified wore down the fabric of equanimity and participation from the dispensation. The implication is to evolve an ideological-institutional mode of moral being in both the worlds, the private and public, and to conquer the pitfalls of self-aggrandizement, which Shashi Tharoor associates with the concept of *dharma*:

> In my view, to live in dharma is to live in harmony with one's purposes on earth, not necessarily in a traditional way. Dharma today must accompany doubt and diversity; it must accept that there is more than one Truth, more than one Right, more than one dharma.[9]

All he wants the readers to share is to recognize the fact that we must have a common enemy to be together, which was in the British rule in a symbolic way, and now, more apparently in our own being. Quoting Theodor Herzl's view of nations as "a historical group of men of recognizable cohesion held together by a common enemy," he holds that "the common enemy of Indians is an internal one."[10] What he embarks upon to examine is the manifestations and syndromes of this eternal internal enemy, wrecking the socio-cultural gains of the freedom movement in a free, democratic India, and to make us participate in a spiritual resurgence, identifying the enemy within ourselves.

When Ved Vyas sets the agenda of his memories before his friend Brahma, saying: "in my epic I shall tell of past, present and future, of existence and passing, of efflorescence and decay, of death and rebirth; of what is, of what was, of what should have been," (18) he goes backwards into recesses of the time to probe the reasons or value-structure of the modern Kurukshetra, the Emergency. It goes without saying that if the old Kurukshetra brought about the philosophy of 'karma' delivered by Lord Krishna, the modern versions of Kurukshetra require all of us to discern and devise the ways and intents of righteousness as self-effacingly as done by the Krishna of modern times, D.K. Parthasarthi, a local MLA, and secretary of the Kaurava Party/ Congress in the novel.

The narrative begins in the princely state of Hastinapur during the British Raj amidst fears of annexation, lurking after the death of Shantanu:

> When kings died without heirs in the days of the Raj, the consequences could be calamitous. Whereas in the past the royal house could simply have adopted a male child to continue the family's hold on the throne, this was not quite as easy under the British, who had a tendency to declare the throne vacant and annex the territory for themselves. (30)

The state of Hastinapur without an heir is typical of the state of Indian freedom movement under the Congress divided into the moderates and the extremists whom the British government did not recognize as the true representatives of the native people. But Ganga Dutta/Gandhi took charge of the affairs in the Congress by installing Dhritarashtra/Jawaharlal Nehru as the heir-apparent to the leadership of the Congress and the nation. Acting regent-like, Gandhi or the mythological Ganga Dutta supervised the direction of the freedom movement and transformed the Congress into a radical force of change with his growing spiritual convictions, as the aide confides to the British Resident Sir Richard:

> He seems to believe in the moral authority, Sir. . . . Untouchability is no longer legal in Hastinapur, . . . But, of late, he has been known to say things about Swaraj. . . . And about pan-Indian nationalism. (37-38)

Gandhi not only gave freedom movement a social objective by including more and more socially discarded people into the mainstream of the national politics, but also nurtured the Congress as the nursery of would-be leaders. Extolling the virtues of Ganga Dutta, the self-conscious narrator, and the *de facto* father of the royal progenies, Ved Vyas says:

> It was, indeed, Gangaji who brought up my sons—as if, I must admit, they were his own children. Though the regent was getting more and more ascetic in his ways, he spared no extravagance in giving the boys the best education, material comforts and personal opportunities. Each developed, in his own way, into an outstanding prospect, a princely asset to Hastinapur. . . .
>
> When he spoke of his intentions to his three young wards, trembling tensely before him at the brink of adulthood, he was not lying or posturing. . . . His truth emerged from his convictions. . . . Truth could not be obtained by 'untruthful,' or unjust or violent means. You can very well understand why Dhritarashtra and Pandu, in their different ways, found themselves, unable to live up to his precept even in his own lifetime. (41, 48)

The creed of Gandhi is meaningful for the process, not the products. He practised, and then called others to join. It is not as if he were following some borrowed text with a professional zeal, and for superficial impression. The narrator's marked reference to the contrasting ways of Gandhi and Gandhians, particularly such as Dhritarashtra/Nehru and Pandu/Subhas calls forth a radical explanation of the Gandhian motto of the justification of ways of truth. Others followed only in principle what Gandhiji practised with his own self. Casting away doubts about the passivity of the Gandhian philosophy of truth, the narrator elaborates:

> Gangaji's truth required activism, not passivity. If you believed in truth and cared enough to obtain it, Ganga affirmed, you had to be prepared actively to suffer for it. It was essential to accept punishment willingly in order to demonstrate the strength of one's convictions. (48)

In fact, the first real experiment with truth came about after the tenure of his regency was over, and he sympathized with the plight of a peasant Rajkumar from a remote district, Motihari, in the British India:

> But what can the dull black-on-white of their textbooks tell them of the heady excitement of those days? of walking through the parched fields to the huts of the poorest men, to listen to their sufferings and tell them of their hopes; of holding public hearings in the villages, where peasants could come forth and speak for the first time of their lives, to people who would do something about it; of openly defying the indigo laws, as Ganga himself wrenched free the first Indigo plant and sowed a symbolic fistful of grain in its stead. (50-51)

Gandhi's values emerged from his convictions of justice and liberty for the existence of man, and his crusade thereby implied sacrifice and suffering to make others believe in the truth he demonstrated. As Ved Vyas says:

> All this was not just morally right. . . . Where sporadic terrorism and moderate constitutionalism had both proved ineffective, Ganga took the issue of freedom to the people as one of simple right and wrong—law versus conscience and gave them a method to which the British had no response. By abstaining from violence, he wrested the moral advantage. By breaking the law non-violently, he showed up the injustice of the law. By accepting the punish-

ments the law imposed on him he confronted the colonialists with their own brutalization. (55)

If the Second Book "Duel with the Crown" puts forth how Mahatma Gandhi proves the weapons of morality and truth superior to the weapons of violence, the Third shows his determination to persist with it even in the face of opposition. The Bibigarh massacre, a variant of the twentieth-century Jallianwalla Bagh massacre, only united the entire nation to face the might of the empire together:

> The massacre and its reward made Indians of us all, Ganapathi. It turned loyalists into nationalists and constitutionalists into revolutionaries. . . . He now saw freedom as indivisible from Truth, and he never wavered again in his commitment to ridding India of the evil empire. (83)

The entry of Dhritarashtra and Pandu into the national politics is interpreted contrastively as having one creed but two different callings. Their personalities came in the way of the total realization of Gandhian principles:

> Dhritarashtra's disappointment with fatherhood and the failing health of his grim wife drove him whole-heartedly into politics. . . . He had the blindman's gift of seeing the world not as it was, but as he wanted it to be. . . . Gangaji, the party's political and spiritual mentor, made no secret of his preference for the slim and confident young man.
>
> Nor for Pandu the flights of fancy of his sightless sibling, nor, for that matter, the ideological flirtations, the passionate convictions, the grand sweeping gestures of principle that became the hallmarks of Dhritarasthra's political style. Pandu believed in taking stock of reality. . . . His duties as the party's chief organizer were indirectly responsible for his political differences with Dhritarashtra. The process of building up a party structure and a cadre committed to run it in the teeth of colonial hostility convinced him that discipline and organization were far greater virtues than ideas and doctrines. It was the classic distortion, Ganapathi, . . . the elevation of means over ends, of methods over aspirations. (85-86)

The incompatibility between means and ends continued to dog the two proteges, which is harnessed by the mentor productively but not for long "when his grip began to slip." (86)

In the Book "The Rains Came" and "The Raj Quartet," the disappointment of Dhritarashtra over the birth of a girl and Pandu's tacit approval of his wives having progenies from extra-marital relationships show their over-enthusiasm to perpetuate their hold on power through their lineage, which vainly ends with the annexation of Hastinapur. However, Ganga Dutta moves on relentlessly with a broader mission of fight for the rights of the underprivileged and exploited. After Motihari, it is Budge Budge in West Bengal where indigenous jute industry workers were being underpaid. As Ved Vyas reminisces on the Gandhian leadership:

> Ganga represented the wise, disinterested leadership the workers had yearned for, but his disinterest was also its own disqualification asserting his moral principles, by upholding abstract canons of Truth and justice, he was laying nothing more than his beliefs on the line. While they were, if their starvation continued, laying down their lives. (99)

Notwithstanding the contradiction of self-sacrifice, the unbecoming liaison and co-operation of the sister of the mill-owner, Sarah Moore, proves the universal dimension of Gandhian motto:

> Sarah understood Gandhi intuitively. It was one of the odder mysteries of Indian history that the person who most quickly got on to Ganga's instinctive wavelength was not one of us from Hastinapur, who had found his eccentricities so difficult, but this English bourgeoisie. (102)

It is during this encounter with the British system that Ganga Dutta discovers the strength of fasting:

> In fasting, in directing the strength of his convictions against himself, Gangaji taught us to resist injustice with arms that no one could take away from us. Gangaji's use of the fast made our very weakness a weapon. . . . He had realized that the best way to bring

> his principles to life was, paradoxically, by being prepared to die for them. (105)

The roles of Dhritarashtra and Pandu were not as overwhelmingly successful as one would expect them to be. Gandhi was alone behind most of his politically strategic victories. The public success of Ganga Dutta's/Gandhi's inner conviction represents his single-minded quest for achieving unity with the masses of India. He immediately identifies with the sufferings of the people and rises above to symbolize its cause through persistence, persuasion, and the power of conscience. Satyagrah through undertaking fast and peaceful protest becomes his time-tested weapons, which he uses with courage, conviction and fortitude. But Dhritarashtra and Pandu, working to 'propel Gangaji's vision into a tangible nationhood,' act to make the Kaurava Party/Congress to be their personal fiefdom and fall apart:

> I watched them both my flawed and gifted sons; . . . I saw the inevitability of their separation. Pandu became impatient of Dhritarashtra's oratorical certitudes, his lofty convictions and vaulting ambition. Dhritarashtra, in turn, had little time for Pandu's atavistic traditionalism, his political earthiness. (112)

This development took place because "Gangaji's spectacularly unorthodox successes had shaken up the verities of the party's post and opened it up for capture." (111) But Ganga Dutta/ Gandhi carries on "as oblivious as always to the dilemmas of other doing nothing to heal the growing rift." (113) If the decision to send Ganga Dutta as the lone representative of the Kaurava Party to the Viceroy's conference reflects the presumptuous stance of Dhritarashtra, the success of the Mango March, which united Indians of all shades and corners, regions and religions, bears out the scepticism of Pandu. Apparently the values of sacrifice, suffering, identity of purpose, truth, non-violence, honesty and selflessness that Ganga Dutta/Gandhi practises as a political ideology are preached only theoretically or governed only mechanically by the two budding leaders of the nation respectively. They never reconcile to the unity of purposes. Nor have they any practical way-out to the institutionalization of the self-sustained methodology of Gandhi. While the Kaurava Party, under the tutelage of Ganga Dutta surges ahead measuring up to the guile of the British imperialism, the cause of Muslim Group led by Mohammed Ali Karna/Jinnah becomes amenable to the British in forestalling the nationalist resurgence:

> The strategy was amoral, the tactics immoral. The obvious cleavage to strike upon was between the 'Hindus' and the 'Muslims.' It mattered little that such terms themselves (concealing as they did so many complex divisions and identities) made little sense, not that they covered groups which had never, in all of India's political history, functioned as monoliths. It mattered little, because Indians proved only too willing to echo Britain's political illiteracy and agree to be defined in terms imposed upon them by their conquerors. (135)

Mohammed Ali Karna's alienation from the mainstream of national politics is due to his formal and clinical perception about the British system, favouring "the terms of the law, familiarity with British constitutional jurisprudence, and parliamentary practice,' and because of what Dhritarashtra terms his prejudices against the masses. His reservations against Hinduism are also marked as Ved Vyas says: "It was not Islam that separated him from Gangaji, but Hinduism." (142) Though he terms Ganga Dutta and his Kaurava Party as "the only actors of any consequence on the stage," he believes them standing for "all that is retrogressive and populist in Indian politics." (145) Clearly, all these prejudices and absence of a truly rational mechanism put the nationalist movement at cross-roads:

> The Kaurava Party, riven by the dissent of the Panduites, its most successful popular movement of civil disobedience suspended in the wake of Chaurasta deaths, its eccentric charismatic leader continuing to thumb his nose at the Raj. And in the opposite corner, the Muslim Group, richly endowed, favourably looked upon by the rulers, decisively led. The clash was inevitable as its outcome was uncertain. (148)

Despite opposition and rancour, Ganga Dutta does "little to change the pattern at the top, where a handful reigned, derided, as 'party bosses' by the British and hailed as 'people's leaders' by the Kauravas." (172) Ganga Dutta is not tolerant of Pandu's rise to the presidentship of the Kaurava Party, as he does not approve of his methods. He brings moral pressure on Pandu through unremitting correspondences and public outcry forcing him to resign. Holding Gandhi responsible for divisiveness and dissension, Pandu addresses a peasant rally thus:

> Divisiveness and disloyalty do not flourish in the bright heat of the sun, they grow in the shade afforded them by the leafy boughs of an old banyan tree. (172)

The very fact that Ganga Dutta/Gandhi had the last say in the monolithic functioning of the Kaurava Party/Congress alienating many did not let true democracy take roots. Gandhi was good so far as enlightening the masses about their socio-cultural concerns and civic responsibilities required his unique spiritual ardour. But he had his reservations in accommodating dissent, difference and decisions other than what he wanted. He became synonymous with the party and did not approve of multiplicity of views. As a result, the values of self-righteousness, truth, honesty, tolerance, co-existence and compassion, which he espoused in the personal capacity failed to signify in the structure of the party and society. In spite of all the goodness and appeal he held for the people in his individual capacity, he hardly succeeded in enshrining them in the body politic because of certain predilections, limitations and presuppositions. Naturally, his values became his own trap of existence reflected in his failure in averting the Muslim group from resorting to 'Direct Action' for a separate land for the Muslims:

> Gangaji refused to be reconciled to the new reality. He walked in vain from riot-spot to riot-spot, trying to put out the conflagration through expressing of reason and grief. But the old magic was gone. . . . It was almost as if the Mahaguru and his message had only touched a corner of the national consciousness, a corner re-

> served for the higher attributes of conscience and historical memory, but one unrelated to the dictates of reality or the needs and constraints of the present. (211)

Facing 'the acid test' of reality, as Dhritarashtra pleaded with Gangaji, "the Working Committee of the Kaurava Party resolved unanimously to accept in principle the partition of the country," (223) going against the expressed wishes of Gangaji. Ganga Dutta dies a victim to his own vow in the wake of the Partition riots and his assassin is none other than his own creed of forced self-contentment and spiritual consummation which he tried to uphold for public good, incarnated as Amba/Shikhandin/Godse. In his obituary, Ved Vyas laments: "What I feel about Gangaji can't be put into words, and in a sense everything I have been telling you, and everything we are living today, is the Mahaguru's funeral oration." (234)

The post-Partition India marks a significant occasion in the nation's history with the birth of Draupadi Mokrasi or democracy. If the pre-Partition India shows how Ganga Dutta's life becomes a living experiment with truth or the concept of freedom and consequent inability to sustain it in the face of the imperatives of power, the post-Partition India calls for examining its tryst with democracy. Tharoor's exposition of Gandhian values of freedom is as much critically constructive as his observations on the development of democracy in a free, sovereign set-up. Gandhi symbolized the democratic process but failed to crystallize it as a product. Democracy meant a popular system of faith and governance through participation, enshrining the same values with which the freedom struggle was started under the leadership of Ganga Dutta/Gandhi. With Dhritarashtra as the presiding deity of the nation, Tharoor examines the sons of Pandu. The fact that she (Draupadi) is the bone of contention and the catalyst for the battle of Kurukshetra gives the novelist the perspective to probe the parallels of misadventure and misalignment.

The birth of democracy in India itself has been shown as an unethical consequence of the premature amalgamation of the 1935 Westminster model of Constitution with Indian aspirations, symbolically drawn through the liaison between Dhritarashtra/ Nehru and Lady Drewpad/Edina Mountbatten:

> At last, on 26 January 1950, as the constitution of the new Republic of India was solemnly promulgated by its founding fathers, Georgina Drewpad, her face awash with tears, delivered herself of a squalling, premature baby . . . she was to be adopted; neither of her natural parents could openly acknowledge the intimacy that had produced her . . . the baby was called Draupadi . . . and she took the uncouth patronymic of her adoptive father, Mokrasi. (244)

With clear reference to the Indian Constitution drafted by B.R. Ambedkar, she starts her journey giving valuable insights on her treatment, particularly by the so-called custodians. As the narrator sets the agenda of her journey among the free people of India, he looks back in a process of self-renewal:

> The India of which Dhritarashtra assumed the leadership on 15 August 1947 had just been through a cathartic process of regeneration, another stage in the endless cycle. . . . Throughout this unpredictable and often painful process of self-renewal, despite the abrupt stops and starts of the cosmic cycle, the forces of destiny remain unshaken in their purpose. . . .
>
> The vehicles of human politics seem to run off course, but the site of the accident turns out to have been the intended destination.
>
> . . . So it was in our story: Gangaji died, his assassin was hanged, Karnistan was hacked off the stooped shoulders of India, Dhritarashtra attained the prime ministry of a land rocked with chaos and carnage, and out of this all, Draupadi Mokrasi was born, cried and, not without struggle, grew up—into an admirable beautiful, complicated, desirable . . . creature whose life gives meaning to the rest of the story. (245-46)

In the accession of Manimir/Kashmir to India in 1948, Dhritarashtra's/ Nehru's creed of idealism and manipulation is further highlighted:

> The state whose attachment to India was the most eloquent possible repudiation of the religious Partition paid a high price for Dhritarashtra's idealism. . . . It was also over Manimir that Dhritarashtra first revealed the technique of political self-perpetuation. . . .

> He knew perfectly well that with Gangaji gone and Pandu dead, Karna across the new frontiers and Rafi sidelined by the fact that much of his community had suddenly become foreigners, there was no obvious alternative leader the party could find. (261)

A new plot of triangular axis, Priya Duryodhani-Draupadi Mokrasi-the five Pandu sons, emerges as one moves to the national politics. Priya Duryodhani/Indira Gandhi grows up in the shadow of her father, learning the lessons of "the consequences of idealism and the impossibility of individual will" as the official hostess. The Pandavas—Yudhishtir/Morarji Desai, Bhim/the Army, Arjun /the Press, Nakul/The Administrative Services, and Sahdev/the Diplomatic Service, with a "rare heritage and unusual education," decide to follow their father and their teacher Jayaprakash Drona in cultivating politics. Draupadi/Democracy, the centre of post-Partition politics, has, as one of her teacher-appreciators says, the prospects of 'muddling through.' With Dhritarashtra being increasingly wooed by a well-wisher like V. Kanika Menon who calls Jayaprakash Drona 'the saintly anarchist,' the battle-lines are clearly drawn. As Dhritarashtra grows conscious of the threat posed by Drona and his cronies of socialist plank, he seeks advice from Kanika:

> Some people have been advising me that Drona and his young followers are becoming too popular. They feel I ought to be doing something to make life little difficult for them. Cut them down to size. (270)

The long incantatory verse, which renders Kanika's political insight of the traditional treatises like the *Arthashastra* and the Shantiparvan of the *Mahabharata* amusingly to Dhritarashtra, appeals most to Priya Duryodhani:

> A king must always show his might even 'gainst kith and kin; it doesn't matter if he's right. But he must be seen to win. (271)

"She was glad," says Ved Vyas, "that her idealistic father had some less idealistic friends." (273) Power manipulation and dissent suppression henceforth become the hallmarks of the political life of the nation. The virtual elimination of the five pillars of the nation in the decimation of the Pandavas might have given a fillip to Priya Duryodhani's political ambition, which she nearly succeeds in realizing. But the timely intervention of Vidur/ Sardar Patel, the gracious secretary of the Home Ministry, who remains above petty politics and serves the nation with individual foresight, saves the situation. About the general state of affairs under Dhritarashtra's dispensation, Ved Vyas says:

> In Delhi blind Dhritarashtra rules with Priya Duryodhani by his side, and he pledged the nation not so much to the gas and hot water of his Fabian preceptors but to the smoke and steam of the modern industrial revolution their ancestors had denied his country . . . factories sprang up amidst the mud and thatch of our people's homes. Institutions of higher learning . . . mushroomed in the dark humid forests of our ignorance . . . our medical schools produced the most gifted doctors in the hospitals of London while whole districts ached without aspirin . . . our institutes of technology generously subsidized by our tax revenues to churn out brilliant graduates for the research laboratories of American Corporation. (293-94)

Meanwhile the Dhritarashtra-Kanika duo develops the political rhetoric of 'non-alignment' in the international relationships, particularly in the light of the cold war between two power blocs—the USA and the USSR—which has, apart from its concept of neutrality and co-existence, a clandestine cover-up for the dual, paradoxical orientation of the confused body politic:

> To the bluff and amoral slavers and statists on the other side, India's rhetoric was insincere, either a Brahminical ploy to conceal the brown Britishness of their language and education, or a canny camouflage for the capitalist course being pursued beneath India's veneer of democratic socialism. (295)

Duality of approach and confusion continue as both the leaders fail to implement the doctrine and even display a craze for populism and bravado, visible in the annexation of Goa/Comea:

> Both—Dhritarashtra for idealistic reasons, Kanika for ideological reasons—believed in the non-alignment they preached, but neither

> could control the convictions or even the conduct of those who were to implement their policies. Nor could either control indefinitely his own desire to flex the nation's muscles. (295)

The values of unrealistic politics—populism, opportunism, duality, complacency and earning sympathy for self-inflicted wounds—come to the fore as they make India an unwitting prey to the rhetoric of the mixed economy on the home front and Indo-China War in 1962. The values which Pandit Nehru and V.K. Menon symbolized were far off the grassroot realities of India, and a nation's craving for the real strengthening of its people from its own resources without the semblance of chicanery and procrastination. That was being done for self-perpetuation as is demonstrated by the poll success for the third time in a row under Dhritarashtra:

> The year after Comea, Dhritarashtra went to the polls for the third time since independence in the quinquennial exercise that affirmed our status as the world's largest democracy, and triumphed handsomely. (302)

But that the values sustained by opportunity and self-delusion are fraught with dire consequence is as much borne out by the defeat of the nation by the Chakras/Chinese as by the gradual decline of Dhritarashtra from the life of political activity to that of renunciation:

> That was not the most important price the nation had to pay for its defeat by the Chakras. Dhritarashtra, the Dhritarashtra of the confident rhetorical flourishes and dazzling visual metaphors, the Dhritarashtra of the original international initiatives and the high priest of proud non-alignment, would never be the same again. The military humiliation not only shattered his self-esteem; it broke his heart. (305)

In the Book "The Act of Free Choice," it is perspicuous enough that Dhritarashtra/Nehru has no legacy or values for the democratic set-up of India: "Dhritarashtra has left you nothing in his will." (310) For the first time since its birth, it is to act of free choice to decide its destiny as sacredly as the vow of marriage. It is here that the power struggle to choose her groom or fate-signifier becomes apparent within the Kaurava Party between Priya Duryodhani and the dissident Pandavas (Mrs. Gandhi and the Group personifying the five pillars of democracy—the political wisdom, the army, the press, the administrative services and the foreign service). Despite Priya Duryodhani's personal interest in marrying Draupadi off to Ekalavya, an amorous adventurer and low caste by birth, who can be easily manoeuvred as a poverty-stricken philanderer, Draupadi Mokrasi chooses Arjuna as her groom. But, ironically, she is to be shared by the entire Pandava fraternity because of the sacred Panduite injunction of discipline and organization, vividly presented through Kunti Yadav's maternal ruling.

In the aftermath of Dhritarashtra's death, Shishu Pal/Lal Bahadur Shastri makes a good Prime Minister "in his decent and well-meaning way" (317) and teaches Karnistanis/Pakistanis a lesson by inflicting severe military humiliation. He, however, becomes unscrupulous victim to the reverse paradox of Dhritarashtra, wanting peace against winning war and placing "the preservation of life above the exaction of revenge." (318) When Priya Duryodhani is installed as the third Prime Minister of independent India for reasons of her docility, maneuverability and stature, and the Kaurava Party/Congress retains power in "the absence of any real alternative," (339) losing seats all over the country to "a motley array of opposition groups," the dissidence from the eldest Pandava arises in a situation of stocktaking within the Kaurava Working Committee: "If we had stronger leadership, this would not have happened." (339) The acrimonious war between Priya Duryodhani/ Indira Gandhi and Yudhishtir/ Morarji Desai over putting the Kaurava house in order is finally resolved with the traditionalist bias of playing safe and maintaining the *status quo* by making Yudhishtir the Deputy Prime Minister.

Again, in a repeat of Dhritarashtra's political action of resigning from the government in the states on the moral ground of not supporting the British government's undemocratic decision of going to World War II, Yudhishtir resigns on the ground that he is not made party to a Cabinet meeting. As Ved Vyas, acting like Vidur/Sardar Patel to Yudhishtir, says, "An empty seat never benefits the one who has vacated it." The question of transferring the hold of nation in the autocratic hands might well have been avoided but for the manner of Dhritarashtra that gives high moral ground to the individual. It gives Priya Duryodhani a free hand to "promote her cause within the party," (343) and rally against what she calls the reactionary elements among the Kauravas. Priya Duryodhani utilizes the services of a hard-core socialist Ashwathaman/Chandrashekhar to abolish the privy purses of the erstwhile princely states breaking the promise. She also achieves the nationalization of Banks for fostering her socialist credentials to win public acclaim, without taking the majority of the Working Committee into confidence:

> The majority of the working committee went along with her . . . it was better in the popular eye to be associated with a broken promise than with the defence of privilege. Today we all realize what some of us realized even then that nationalization only means transferring functioning and successful institutions from the hands of competent capitalists to those of bumbling bureaucrats. . . . But in those days our Ashwathamans did not speak of profit or loss: they spoke of service. . . . Duryodhani—failing this time to carry a majority of the working committee with her—gave it her personal support and called for a free vote in the House. In the absence of a party whip . . . and with the support of the leftist Opposition parties, woolly-headed socialists and clear-thinking Communists alike, the Bank Nationalization bill was passed. (345-48)

Both of her legislative victories show her personal clout to the detriment of the democratic process and faith. The first one leads to the resignation of Yudhishtir, a prominent Kaurava Party Working Committee member, and the second one, beset by conflict and controversy, to the death of a scrupulous figurehead of the nation, Dr. Mehrban Imandar/Dr. Zakir Hussain. The next strategy on her part is to choose an obliging figurehead of the nation in Shri Ekalavya/V.V. Giri, very much against the official candidate of the party, and on a trivial question of the Bank nationalization, to divide "the great Kaurava Party, the world's oldest anti-colonial political organization, sixteen years away from its centenary." (351) With her catchy and brilliantly coined slogan of 'Remove Poverty,' she not only counters the 'Remove Duryodhani' campaign of the Kaurava (O), but comes to the House with "the recumbent forms of newly elected supplicants" in "a bigger parliamentary majority than even Dhritarashtra had ever enjoyed." (351) The most opportune moment in her political career, however, is the occasion of Gelabi Desh War/Bangladesh War, in which she intervenes because of the imperative "to resolve the deadlock, ease the refugee burden on her soil and in the process teach Karnistan the kind of lesson India itself had to learn not so long ago from Chakra." (355) It is, as Ved Vyas's oneric narrative of the Rajasuya Yajna suggests, to glorify and invest her with an aura of political invincibility: "She was not just deified, she was maternalized." (355)

The political well-being of Priya Duryodhani nevertheless does not augur well for the well-being of the people of India, whose life remains unchanged with the realities of poverty, illiteracy, exploitation, disease and so on because of "the heartless ineptitude of the one in whom they had placed their trust." (356) Unresponsive to the call of duty, she engages herself in paying lip service to the cause of the masses with socialist rhetoric and acquires more and more power as reward. She dismembers the press, fetters the judiciary and emasculates representative democracy in her own party on the pretext of its being out of touch with the masses. It touches the pinnacle of whimsical assault on the body politic. Ved Vyas says:

> While the poor remained as poor as they had ever been while striking trade unionists were beaten and arrested, while peasant demonstrations were assaulted and broken, all this while more and more laws went on to the statute books empowering Priya Duryodhani to prohibit, proscribe, profane, prolate, prosecute, or prostitute all the freedoms the national movement had fought to attain during all those years of my Kaurava life. (357)

The inescapable fall-out of this autocratic syndrome is the suppression of civic rights and democratic freedom, censuring and authoritarianism, and all that stand against the principles, which enlivened the party during freedom struggle. In her identity, she consumes the nation as well as the party. The values of tolerance, co-existence, sacrifice, and fortitude are disregarded to promote a reign of personal likes and dislikes. In short, it represents a total failure of the democratic process.

Jayaprakash Drona/Jayaprakash Narayan, who leads a popular uprising against her, preaches "not only against Duryodhani but against all the evils she had failed to eradicate, and therefore, in his eyes, had herself come to represent" (363): Venality and corruption, police brutality and bureaucratic inefficiency, rising prices and falling stocks in the shops, adulteration and black-marketing, shortages of everything from cereals to jobs, caste discrimination and communal hatred, neglected births and dowry deaths. With the Kaurava (O) and other parties active, the people's uprising represents a paradox of value-sustained waste, and counter-initiatives. Ved Vyas reflects:

> I was no admirer of Priya Duryodhani or what she stood for, but I was equally distraught about Drona's Popular Uprising and where it was leading the government. . . . For the government to be devoting all its attention to policing opposition rather than developing the country was tragic. For our precious independence to be reduced to anarchy, betrayal and chaos was downright criminal. . . . Drona and Yudhishtir could have rallied the opposition around them, consolidated their organization and swept Duryodhani from power at the hustings. (364)

In the midst of this political crisis, Priya Duryodhani faces a conviction from 'an excessively legalistic provincial court' / Allahabad H'gh Court for sharing an election platform with President Eklavya/V.V. Giri, the figurehead. Fighting with her back to the wall against the demand to quit parliamentary privileges, she persists with the governance by declaring the internal Siege, acting upon the advice of a hand-picked manipulative president of the Kaurava (R) Party/Congress (Indira), Shakuni Shankar

Dey/Siddharth Shakar Ray, and supported by a grateful rubber-stamp President of the nation, Eklavya/V.V. Giri.

In the name of stability and security from internal disruption, a state of anarchy is let loose and legalized: "Not to mention censorship of the press, which is nowhere explicitly ruled out in the Constitution, suspension of certain fundamental rights—free speech, assembly, that sort of thing—and measures to put the judiciary in their place." (366) But for her penchant for earning international credit for the show of democracy, and escaping the opprobrium of "the world's largest banana republic," she surprises everyone by calling free general elections "at the peak of her regime of repression." (389) Musing over the chance to choose between democracy and dictatorship in free elections, Ved Vyas observes the similarity with the freedom struggle:

> I saw the meaning of Independence come pulsating to life as unlettered peasants rose in the villages to pledge their votes for democracy. I saw journalists younger than the constitution relearn the meaning of freedom by discovering what they had lost when the word was erased from their notebooks. I saw Draupadi's face glowing in the open. (392)

It is a battle of ballots, but also a battle between *dharma* and *adharma*, good and evil, and similar to Kurukshetra where there are no real victors with everyone losing at the end. But, all the same, people at large for the first time exercise their rights "to vote on their subjugation." (391) The human existence becomes bereft of every possible freedom in the post-Partition era and there is general gloom on account of suspension of human rights in a native system of governance. There is a long discourse between Krishna and Arjuna/the Press, typical of the *Gita* of Kurukshetra, enjoining upon Arjuna to side with the opposition and fight against the reign of repression: "If you don't fight now you won't have anything to write about afterwards." (393) Arjun resolves:

> I was silly to be irresolute
> Instead of thinking of the spirit

And acting without heed to merit,
I'd wept and whined like a broken flute
That's all over now ! I'm ready to act—
Let's get the opposition into an electoral pact! (398)

In a battle in which everyone takes sides including Yudhishtir/ Morarji Desai (the political protégé of Jai Prakash Narayan as well as inheritor of the Gandhian legacy) and Arjun, the Janata Front, a composition of the entire opposition, encases upon the wrath of the people against Priya Duryodhani, and is voted to power. Nevertheless, to choose a new Prime Minister consensually from among so many constituents revives the old fear of Dhritarashtra-Pandu tussle—the tussle between populism and principles. Taking a leaf out of the history's book, the mentors of the new victorious Front—Jayaprakash Drona/ Jayaprakash Narayan and Ved Vyas declare Yudhishtir, the honest, sincere and senior, as the moral choice for the nation's leadership together with the installation of Ashwathaman/Chandrashekhar as the populist president of the party organization. As Ved Vyas narrates the oath-taking to have been ritualized before the Taj, he pays tributes to the land of beauty and grandeur amidst suffering and death, albeit ironically. But the hopes are betrayed again as "within weeks of its assumption of office it had become the vehicle for the personal ambitions of at least three veteran politicians besides the Prime Minister." (405) Notably the three veterans referred to are Chowdhury Charan Singh, Jagjivan Ram and Raj Narain. The government Yudhishtir heads begins to crumble with the support of the disgruntled leaders including Ashwathaman. The disappointment of Drona at this development is characteristic of that of Gangaji, as "he lay torn between loyalty to the government he had created and the son for whom he had, all those years ago, changed his life." (408) In order to muster support for his leadership, Yudhishtir manipulates the lie of Ashwathaman's death that tragically brings about Drona's death, and endorses his plea for unity: "I may not have spoken the whole truth, but I spoke no untruth, and my words may have helped sustain a greater truth by prompting him to endorse my plea for unity. Would it have been better to allow his tremendous moral authority to have been manipulated by the radical rabble to bring down the government that has restored Indian democracy?" (410) Truth comes to prevail although Ved Vyas calls it "too immutable to be uttered only in the letter and violated in the spirit" and Yudhishtir's government falls as "Dharma had turned full circle." (411) In the victory of Truth, "not your truth or mine," Ved Vyas, the narrator, recreates the myth of the *Mahabharata*, where there is destruction for all, and solace for none.

'The Path to Salvation,' the concluding book of the novel, re-creates the scene of Pandavas's journey to Heaven. It is reproduced almost as it is except the final comment of Yudhishtir: "Derive your standards from the world around you and not from a heritage whose relevance must be constantly tested." (418)

In *The Great Indian Novel* as in *Midnight's Children*, there are digressions, fables and anecdotes, which mark departure from the main plot. Although both Saleem and Ved Vyas have an audience/scribe (Padma/Ganapathi) to listen to/record their story, they are self-conscious narrators who are preoccupied with the problems of metafiction, i.e. multiplying fictional parallels of the reality. Tharoor's treatment of the myth of the *Mahabharata* is typical of James Joyce's treatment of the myth of *Odyssey* in *Ulysses* as means of undermining world of Western discourse. It not only explicates a cosmic vision of modern times, but also studies human life and mind.

NOTES

1. J.S. Negi, "Introduction," to U.P. Arora, *Motifs in Indian Mythology* (New Delhi: Munshiram Manoharlal, 1981), p. vi.
2. Paul Ricoeur, "Life in Quest of Narrative," in *On Paul Ricoeur: Narrative and Interpretation*, ed. David Wood (London: Routledge, 1991), pp. 20, 25, 30-31.
3. Milan Kundera, "Dialogue on the Art of Composition," *The Art of the Novel*, trans. Linda Asher (New Delhi: Rupa, 1992), p. 73.
4. Lillian Feder, *Ancient Myth in Modern Poetry*, pp. 10-11.

5. Qtd. Shashi Tharoor, "A Note on *Dharma*," *The Great Indian Novel* (New Delhi: Penguin India, 1989), p. 420.
6. Viney Kirpal, "Politics and Philosophy in *The Great Indian Novel*," *Littcrit*, Vol. 16, nos. 1 and 2, June-December 1990, p. 46.
7. Shashi Tharoor, "Yoking of Myth to History," *Littcrit*, Vol. 16, nos. 1 and 2, June-December 1990, p. 46.
8. Josiah Royce, "The Larger Self," *Readings in Philosophy*, ed. J.H.R. Jr., J.H. Buchler and E.V. Shirk (New York: Barnes and Noble, 1950), p. 366.
9. Shashi Tharoor, *India from Midnight to Millennium* (New Delhi: Penguin India, 1997), p. 358.
10. *Ibid.*, p. 128.

Indian Legacy: The Birth of a New Myth

LUDMILA VOLNÁ
Charles University, Prague

> I dreamt once more of legends past, of shimmering palaces and moustachioed men in shining brass armour and princesses glowing with gold bangles and scented garlands; of glorious Hastinapur, home of my ancestors. (375)

Myths play an important role in the history of man. As contemplations of the ancestors they offer the explanation of the natural and cultural phenomena of the civilization and answers to the enigmas of existence. They constitute the culture's awareness of its past and so its sense of appurtenance, heroic figures and deeds activate the culture's pride and self-respect. Unlike in the West where myths usually may be perceived more as a creation of an individual (at least in their written form), in India legends and myths have been coming into existence as a collective wisdom of a multifold, variable, and ancient civilization. They are also shared collectively in the minds of people. Inherited from ancestors, they have been retold as stories from generation to generation and a great number of variations have been created by the storytellers who have given the legends their individual flavour. Even now in India we can witness public recitations of parts of the great epics, the *Ramayana* and the *Mahabharata*. An endless source of inspiration, they have been reworked by all kinds of art. For novels and films, just as for myths and folktales, it is typical that the fate of the individual is related to the strivings and ambition of the society which brings them close to the literary tradition of the nineteenth century realism. The individual characters work more or less as symbolic mediators of a world greater than that which immediately surrounds them.[1]

Shashi Tharoor's *The Great Indian Novel* (1989) and an earlier work of Salman Rushdie, *Midnight's Children* (1981), are two modern Indian novels written in English which are notably representative of this perspective. They have, however, much more in common, which is indicated already by their titles. 'Midnight' connecting the reference to something magic with the context of India's Independence, 'children' alludes to the history and future of the nation and its legacy at the same time. In Sanskrit, 'Maha' means 'great' and 'Bharata' means 'India'—it is a clear enough allusion to the ancient epic of the *Mahabharata* and so to India's heroic past; the word 'novel' promises perhaps the connection to the present. As Evelyne Hanquart-Turner remarks, "it is 'novel' also insofar as it offers new, and one may add contemporary material, about the story of India as told through the ancient epic."[2] Both Rushdie and Tharoor use the ancient myths and legends of India to make the history of modern India their subject. They create works which are their own but into which the fabric of the myth essence is intrinsically woven, either in a rather straightforward or in a more complex manner. How this is done will be the objective of this article, the extent of which, with respect to the vast complexity of the novels, must nevertheless remain within certain limits. These will not permit more than just a limited number of aspects to be dealt with, the aspects which concern the interrelations between the ancient patterns and the new creations and how the authors work with them to create a new myth from/with the help of the 'materia' of the old one.

Inheritors of the Story

The story is the vehicle-element of both novels. The narrative frame of *The Great Indian Novel* copies that of the ancient *Mahabharata* openly: the character named Ved Vyas is dictating 'his story and that of his times' to the elephant-nosed south-Indian Ganapathi to put it down, the allusion only too obvious to the elephant-headed god Ganesha, who was supposed to take down the old myth. Saleem, the miraculous character, tells the story of *Midnight's Children* and at the same time he puts it in writing. He tells the story to Padma, his companion, whose name refers to the Lotus Goddess. The old myths and legends of India were also both told and written.

The stories of the two novels are told as the stories of the old myths and legends are told. Apart from the universal popularity of the story because it communicates meaning more comprehensible than the language of the abstract and the conceptual, the Indians favour the narrative because of their belief in the ultimate reality, the reality higher than that of the everyday life, the reality, which goes beyond any concept and even beyond mind. The only way to the perception of the ultimate reality is the experiential one, and as such it is best conveyed through myths, folktales, legends, stories, and parables. Aesthetic and mystical experiences are said to be closely related and so in this way the aesthetic power of a well-told tale makes those experiences more rather than less real than life.[3] Indeed, as Saleem says, "some legends make reality and become more useful than the facts." (MC 47)

Now we will have a closer look at how the story is born. In both novels it starts with the birth of its tellers, which reflects the classical Western novel beginnings. The births themselves are particular with regard to time, in which they occur. Ved Vyas was born with the (20th) century, Saleem came into the world exactly on the stroke of midnight 15 August 1947, when India became independent. Saleem's way of describing the circumstances of his birth, i.e. the precise time and place, mirrors the process of giving birth itself. His story is born continuously, with gasps, step by step. Ved Vyas' tale is also born, it is twice born. The first part of the book being entitled as Twice-Born Tale recalls the traditional Hindu idea of the twice-born state of the children (more exactly boys) of the caste Hindus, which means that it is only at the age between five and ten that the child starts to be perceived as a member of the society and also receives some responsibility regarding his behaviour. Because Tharoor's characters are put on the scene as the modern counterparts of the characters of the *Mahabharata* inheriting indeed even their names, it is as if the tale of the old epic is now born for the second time and retold. As if the events of the *Mahabharata* had happened once and now they are repeated and told as the tale of *The Great Indian Novel*. In terms of the present society the 'first' *Mahabharata* is as innocent as a child up to the age of five and it is only now in its 'second' (birth) version, that it acquires meaning and brings forth responsibility.[4]

Having in mind the 'retelling' of the *Mahabharata* as the story of *The Great Indian Novel* we are getting to the phenomenon of 'circularity' or the 'cyclical' quality of the work. The story 'of death and rebirth' alludes to the Hindu life cycle repeated infinitely in order to achieve 'moksha' (the ultimate goal of existence) with 'dharma' (duty carefully prescribed) as its 'vehicle.' In the same way as the Hindus' lives are not believed to really end at the moment of death but to continue somewhere else and result in the next rebirth, "stories never end, they just continue somewhere else." (418) The whole of Ved Vyas's story is being told from the perspective of and with an overwhelming importance paid to dharma. Consequently, his tale is finally cast upon with a crucial doubt. Convinced that he is mistaken, he decides to retell the whole story once more, this time from the 'right' point of view. In this way dharma turns full circle. (411) The outcome, however, is ambiguous: will he tell the story of the same events and with the same set of characters, but a story which would be modified according to his new understanding, or will the story be exactly the same because it cannot be different? (18, 418)

Saleem's story is also repeated as he told it once before and the cyclical aspect is echoed as well in the final outcome of the novel as the vision of a thousand and one generations and a thousand and one midnights. Nevertheless, the circle is not the stories' only 'geometrical' structure. As Ved Vyas insists that he is telling nothing less than the epic "of past, present and future," (18) the triangular structure imposes itself, which is reflecting a similar pattern in *Midnight's Children.* After Saleem's story has been born it struggles its way into the world, supplied mainly by the narrator's memory, all by itself for some time. It is written and at the same time read to Padma, Saleem's companion, and it is through her that the story-activity based on memory is balanced as she and Saleem start to love each other. Finally Saleem himself, whose life is the subject of the story and about whom we have already got to know sufficiently enough, counterbalances the two, that is the memory and Padma, in order to create a triangular structure, reflecting thus the threefold image of Shiva-Trinity of a central, immovable Absolute and two side profiles, the right one of Shiva representing virility and will-power (both are vital for the accomplishment of Saleem's story), the left one of the female principle,[5] both producers and directors of the world spectacle:

> I have become, it seems to me, the apex of an isosceles triangle, supported equally by twin deities, the wild god of memory and the lotus-goddess of the present. (MC 150)

The elements of this triangular structure co-exist further in a sort of symbiosis and interaction. Analogically, each element has some sort of handicap and they all reach a final culmination. First, the story-telling is subjective, based on Saleem's cracking memory, which is continuously more and more fragmentary and subjected to more and more effort to work. The memory's story is finished when there is nothing more left of the past, everything has been told. Second, the love-story is a relationship without consummation, as Padma is not capable of making Saleem's 'other pencil work.' Padma's is 'the present's' contribution to Saleem's story. The love culminates into marriage, but it is a marriage with no hope of future whatsoever. Third, Saleem's body is consumed by widening cracks and rifts, he himself is unable to acquire a positive meaning, though he tries enormously. His life comes to fulfilment only in death. The death has to be foretold as future, the same as the brief outline vision of the nation's future. The reference to the time dimensions of the past, present, and anticipated future in the two novels makes the structure respondent, once again, to that of the Hindu circular perception of time, as a counterpart to the linear one.

Ved Vyas and Saleem are both obsessed with their respective stories, with telling and writing. Both have too many stories to tell. They are put on the scene as the fathers both of the story and of the children who constitute the history, present, and future of India, the 'myth-ridden nation.'[6] What have the story, life, and history in common? The author's story-in-the-novel (story-in-the-story in fact) is nothing less than the structure of the story in which one of the characters starts telling another story in which another character tells still another story, and so on. But what about the characters who did not get the chance to tell their story? And still those who did, did they not have other stories in store that they did not tell? And when the 'end' to a story is proclaimed, what about the future life of the characters? They may be said to 'live happily ever after' but the recipient is perhaps interested in what their future life looked like in more detail. As there is 'no end to the story of life' (163) and because the story has to be selective, in the same way any presentation of history can only choose certain aspects, views, and perspectives. No all-embracing view, no global perspective is possible. It can always be only a kind of distortion.

And that is what the history of the two storytellers is like. Their subject-matter is the history of modern India, the history which starts at the dawn of the century with the circumstances of Ved Vyas's birth, and in Saleem's tale in 1915 when his grandfather came back to Kashmir from Europe, with India gaining Independence as a focus, and covering several more decades. Their history is distorted, errors and irrelevancies occur because it is based on memory, but still it is worth telling. Saleem's memory as well as his body is cracking and history is pouring out of the fissures. He is at great pains to be able to go on and finish. His daily work in the factory where he participates in making chutney by selecting fruits and vegetables and preparing special blends of spices goes hand in hand with the history telling. He is 'conserving' and so preserving history in thirty jars of chutney labelled as the titles of the book chapters. He wants to make his story of history immortal. By referring metonymically to the 'nation' of India, to which he himself is handcuffed by history, in terms of the six hundred million eggs of their origin that could fit in a single jar (while for the six hundred million spermatozoa a single spoon would be sufficient), he is once more bringing the story, history and life together.[7]

But the story of the two narrators is based not only on memory. It is dreams and dreamlike representations, which are not a negligible source in creation of the whole of the tales. Compared to a simple memory-based narrative they are 'marked' and so they play a crucial role in constituting the 'meaning'. As such they occur more towards the end of the novels. Apart from the perception of dream as a counterpart to everyday reality, which in a literary work of art can evoke the relativity of opinion, dream in the Hindu concept relates in the same way to everyday reality as this ordinary reality does to the ultimate reality. That means that the everyday reality (of the story) can be understood through the 'events' or the 'experiences' of the dream (of the story), the concept close enough to that of the 'subconscious' revealed through dream.[8]

The Setting of the Myth Scene

In the *Mahabharata* the Kauravas and the Pandavas, two branches of a ruling family (the descendants of Bharata) fight against each other for the land which eventually, together with other territories, starts to be identified as Bharata. There is dishonesty and greed for power as well as longing for justice together with the wish for the country's best in the old epic and in both its counterparts as they depict modern India's complex and complicated search for self-identification. The process of India coming into existence, though in a different sense, or, in terms of Hindu cosmology, the rebirth of India on an elevated level, is in *The Great Indian Novel* presented as a direct parable of its ancient pattern. The characters, names, actions, motivations, including the instruction and the moral outcome (though the latter is made different by the relativization of an elaborate discussion), all is there. The author of *Midnight's Children* puts on the scene the elements of the *Mahabharata* too: godlike characters—children endowed with supernatural gifts, dubious parentage of the main protagonists, the fight of two rival parties in the matter of 'India'; nevertheless, as a whole the cast of *Midnight's Children* can be perceived as worked out in a complex manner. A large amount of Judaeo-Christian, Islamic, Buddhist, and other kinds of allusion which can be found in both the novels enriches the Hindu tradition with the plurality of a multicultural background.

Let's now have a closer look at the central characters-narrators of the story and their role in the myth-making process. In both works there is an enormous variety of characters who acquire all kinds of heroic or anti-heroic attributes, which, no doubt, qualifies them as mythical (again not only in the Hindu context but also with respect to other faiths; e.g. the Drona character in *The Great Indian Novel* is even called a 'Messiah' [408-9]), but still Ved Vyas's and Saleem's appearances are of the greatest importance. They are telling the story of their life and times, nothing less than the epic

> of past, present and future, of existence and passing, of efflorescence and decay, of death and rebirth; of what is, of what was, of what should have been. (18)

The fact that they both are the storytellers gives once again prominence to the 'institution' of the story. Saleem and Ved Vyas are both the narrators of and the main participants in the events ('epic of my life and times; of past, present, . . . of what is, of what was') and the prophet-like figures who are capable of giving instruction and teaching ('epic of future, . . . of what should have been'); they are capable of influencing the others' lives. Their omniscience, however, clearly fails to be perfect; they are subject to confusion, mistake, and uncertainty, which is significant in the process of search for meaning (see below).

Theirs are enigmatic identities. Ved Vyas's relationship towards India is made closer than that of a 'mere' citizen to the extent that he in a way becomes identified with the country. Characters of the political scene are called at the same time 'his sons' and 'the sons of India.' (115) They owe him not only their origin but often also their actions. A symbolic figure, he stands in the place of the 'forces of destiny.' He arranges the events in the same way as a writer puts together the story of his work. He does it strictly in terms of the moral principles of dharma as presented in the *Mahabharata*. Thus he may be perceived as a principle-creator of the fate of the modern India with respect to his understanding of its dharma. (127, 244-45, 317, 318, 410)

Saleem is also irreversibly bound to the fate of modern India. The analogy is clear—born at the moment of Independence, the events of his childhood and young age and his country's strivings for independent life mirror each other. As soon as he recognizes the miraculous gift inside him, the lives of others as well as all-national events are affected as he pulls the strings, needless to say that he does so in his view in the best interest of India and justice.

Compared to Ved Vyas Saleem is endowed with a much more elaborate parentage. Being born "a bastard, but a bastard in a fine tradition, the offspring of a fisherwoman seduced by a travelling sage," (19) Ved Vyas may represent the not acknowledged yet desirable union of the brahmanic and non-brahmanic cultural traditions of the Indian past. Saleem, the multifold character that he is, shares together with his alter ego Shiva multiple fathers as well as mothers. First, there is a clash between the striving for progress of grandfather Aadam Aziz on one side and Tai's stubborn clinging to the stability and tradition on the other. India's successive process of changing identity is mirrored in Mumtaz Aziz-Khan, Aadam's daughter and Saleem's mother, who becomes Amina Sinai. Among the other parents, e.g. the idealist Nadir Khan, the businessman Ahmed Sinai, and Zulfikar-'the sword' symbolize the varied streams within the Muslim society and the tumult of the changing society. The street singer

Wee Willie Winkie and Picture Singh from the magician ghetto, the Hindus without money yet not without a charm, are made a counterpart to the rich but 'pale' (i.e. colourless) English gentleman Methwold (he has a French predecessor), who is, however, much too great a temptation for the Indian Vanita, Wee Willie Winkie's wife, to resist, the same way as India cannot resist the European cultural impact. Mary (Pereira) and Joseph (da Costa) are another pair of Saleem's parents, clearly alluding to Christianity. Thus the broad spectrum of Saleem-Shiva's parental ancestry—the 'midnight's parents'—represents the legacy of India, all those different voices which are at the origin of the present multicultural Indian reality. Echoing this, 'Midnight's Parents,' the eighth book of *The Great Indian Novel*, emphasizes the multiple character and continuity of a story, and of 'the story of life,' indeed. (121-25)

The Quest for Purpose and Meaning:
Saviours and Prophets Ending in Absurdity?

As has been mentioned both Ved Vyas and Saleem are preoccupied with the meaningful accomplishment of their respective stories and for each of them the writing about the 'life and times' of India is at the same time a relationship of direct mutual influence (between the storyteller and India) and the attempt to save the country. "I must work fast, faster than Scheherazade, if I am to end up meaning—yes, meaning—something. I admit it: above all things, I fear absurdity," (MC 9) Saleem confides in his reader while Ved Vyas feels, "If it means anything, anything at all, it means that I have told my story so far from a completely mistaken perspective. . . . I must retell it." (418)

Saleem starts to realize his confusion about meaning and purpose shortly before his miraculous ability is 'revealed' to him, this being followed by his growing realization that his is not a singular gift but that he has a thousand more prodigious companions of midnight, who all have gifts at their disposal. The search for purpose and meaning called for by Saleem now at the platform of the Midnight's Children Conference acquires a new dimension—a plurality of opinions expressed by the children. At about the same time of real Indian history, the five Pandavas of *The Great Indian Novel* can be found to travel around the country, pursuing justice and altruism and so establishing their reputation as mythical heroes. Intertextuality permits us to see the gifts on both sides as complementary endowments. If in Rushdie's work most of the children are first presented, at least as viewed in their respective environments, as normal human children with usual names, in *The Great Indian Novel* the characters are initially given the names of the old myth figures and so the reader already foresees how their miraculous qualities will manifest themselves. However, it is the children of midnight, whose gifts are presented as really supernatural, magic, though those of the Pandava characters are described in terms of representing 'the political legacy; the army; the spirit of the Indian people both in its diversity and discordance, doubts and questions; the administration and diplomatic services'; all of these supposed to be united by their common wife Draupadi, who stands for the principle of democracy. (292-93, 319-21)

Whereas in *Midnight's Children* the question of meaning vs. absurdity is evoked once the setting is established, the events of the new myth of *The Great Indian Novel* seem to flow forward throughout the whole novel quite in accordance with the old myth's characters' doings. "This is our dharma," (245) says Ved Vyas, father and storyteller, yet the representative of the 'Old Guard.' In *Midnight's Children* the quest for modernity starts already with Aadam Aziz, a counterpart of the boatman Tai; *The Great Indian Novel* presents Ved Vyas as a symbol of the dharma principle who arranges both the events and the story within the limits of this unmovable Hindu law, thus standing for the tradition and old ways; there is no real counterpart to this state of matters until the very end of the work. But when finally one of the characters, Yudhishtir, the one who is the most perseverant, speaks up and challenges the god Dharma, his own father, what comes out may seem, however, a little ambiguous. First, it all happens in Ved Vyas's dream. Second, the scene of the dream is set as afterlife of the characters. On the other hand the two objections can be easily rooted out, not only on the simple presumption that two relativizations-negatives give one positive, but mainly because, first, what Ved Vyas introduces as dreams in his story is put in direct connection with what is described in the form of common events. Second, the scene of afterlife continues copying the pattern of the original *Mahabharata*, only the outcome is different. Rather, the manner in which this outcome is presented by the author may be his way to stress its importance in comparison with what has been said until now. Yudhishtir's appeal against the rigid tradition and for the benefit of plurality, tolerance and newness not only extinguishes the god Dharma, but has such an impact on Ved Vyas himself that he decides his story has been told from a completely mistaken perspective. The new myth is once again made absurd or negative through the influence of the old one. The story must be now retold in a new way.

Absurdity has to be faced: the miracle has gone wrong. The clash of the issues of 'ideas' and 'things' is represented by a multiple xenophobic argument as an expression of the state of political affairs of young India; on a larger scale it reflects the human situation with its 'man-made' problems in general. The void becomes the turning point between meaning and absurdity. The absence of something new and forgetfulness of the 'new myth of freedom' brings about the awakening of the old myth of the *Mahabharata* which comes haunting with its war fields where lots of human talents were lost in the struggle for the shape of the country coming into existence. (MC 245) The old myth's legacy makes the new myth become a negative, absurd mythical creation. Before the 'saviours' can succeed in their efforts, long, repeated periods of time, of birth and rebirth are necessary to be accomplished, which is due, from the cosmological point of view, to the influence of Kali-yuga, the last and the most corrupted stage of a world cycle.[9]

The Meaning through Writing

If the myth has gone wrong in the perspective of both Ved Vyas's and Saleem's lives because their 'mission to save the country' during their respective lifetimes remained unfulfilled the writers-creators let their heroes—representatives and fathers of the miraculous generation—succeed on a different level. Though Saleem-saviour fails in person then and Ved Vyas's puppets get out of his hands because for both it is beyond their power to master the fate, both of them accomplish a kind of 'meaning' through the 'letters'. Their writing acquires the form of a 'code' containing both the description and the explanation of the situation, both the crisis, and the instruction how to cope with it.

Saleem as a would-be-saviour claims the central place in the course of the events (MC 238); yet he admits that this is not the only centre focus.

> Women have fixed me all right, but perhaps they were never central—perhaps the place which they should have filled, the hole in the centre of me which was my inheritance from my grandfather Aadam Aziz, was occupied for too long by my voices . . . the hole at the centre of himself caused by his (which is also my) failure to believe or disbelieve in God.[10]

Ved Vyas's central position in the narrative is more than obvious, yet he too feels there is a failure.

Clearly this can be perceived as a 'negative meaning,' absurdity, emptiness. There is a 'failure' and there is a 'hole'. But it is so only because, as we have seen, the old beliefs or disbeliefs are no more relevant and must be replaced, or reformulated. Saleem by making errors and by relying on his 'unreliable' memory makes the view of the absolute Truth relative. As in the case of the tetrapod, which was viewed by different people either as a 'technological miracle' or as Shiva-lingam, points of view may be as varied as the scale between a 'snake' and a 'ladder' (expressing the oppositions, or polarities) (MC 141) and as many as the 'whirlpool of multitudes.' (MC 463) In *The Great Indian*

Novel, Ved Vyas, depending in his acts and writing firmly on the traditional laws of dharma, finds out in the end that he was telling his story from a completely mistaken perspective and therefore has to rewrite it. Whether he is able to do it remains a question because he starts his new story with exactly the same words as the original one. Perhaps the time has not yet come for it to be possible and a lot of attempts have to be made by many further generations of Ved Vyases before it can be accomplished. Nevertheless, the outcome is clear, there is 'not one truth, no classical verities valid for all time.'[11]

Viney Kirpal writes: "according to Rushdie, the form represents the very basis of Indian art which is pluralistic. It has got to do with "the combining of many different ways of looking. And if you select one of those ways of looking you make a false picture. That influenced me in the writing of *Midnight's Children*."[12]

The pluralistic basis manifests itself already through the numberless different representations of Indian myths, no matter whether fixed as literature or transmitted orally. Both in *Midnight's Children* and in *The Great Indian Novel* the pluralistic character is reflected in the structure as many multicultural elements are employed by both authors as, for example, Hanquart-Turner observes for *The Great Indian Novel:*

> The foreign element in the plot is then tackled through multicultural sources; to the weft of the Indian antic myths, Tharoor adds the warp of colonial and postcolonial fiction which echoes throughout the first ten books of the novel.[13]

Plurality and multicultural view is the core of the outcome of both novels. With respect to the way the subject matter is treated the two novels appear rather 'complementary' to each other. Whereas *Midnight's Children* can be perceived as more complex and refers more to the cosmic level of the myth when presenting the historical condition of modern India, the author of *The Great Indian Novel* chooses a more linear approach for his reflection.

The conflict of meaning and absurdity in this *Mahabharata* retold is resolved then in a rather straightforward manner.

In both novels analogical 'meaning through writing' is being conveyed by their storytellers. As to the fulfilment of their "dual lust for fathers and saving-the-country," they are no more 'puppeteers' but rather "puppets with broken strings" (MC 262, 426) and as such they are unable to save the country through any immediate personal action. The fulfilment and meaning is to be accomplished rather by the search for fathers. The search not for one, but for as many fathers as possible. It is a search for roots which are not defined by just one culture or religion but by many, as supported by numerous allusions. The 'hole' of belief/disbelief is to be filled with a different structure, that of the enlightenment. The rigidity of old beliefs is to be abandoned for the benefit of plurality of multiple roots and opinions.[14]

Thus the new myth and its quest for meaning as viewed in the cosmological perspective of Hinduism, supported by numerous allusions to other traditions and by their imageries, becomes the appeal for plurality, tolerance and change as opposed to the totality of opinion, prejudice, and one-sided rigorous sticking to the principles of tradition. Basic all-human qualities are stressed because they unite people contrary to the totalitarian ideologies and ultimate truths which divide them. There is finally hope for that highly vital community of 'India, which is eternal,' (418) to emerge again from the 'whirlpool of multitudes.' (MC 463)

NOTES

1. Heinrich Zimmer, *Myths and Symbols in Indian Art and Civilization* (1946; Princeton, New Jersey: Princeton University Press, 1992), 39-41. Sudhir Kakar, *The Inner World* (1981; Delhi-Bombay-Calcutta-Madras: Oxford University Press, 1996), 4. Sudhir Kakar, *Intimate Relations: Exploring Indian* Sexuality (1989; New Delhi: Penguin India, 1990), 2, 4.
2. Evelyne Hanquart-Turner, "Echoes, Palimpsests and Transmutations in Shashi Tharoor's *The Great Indian Novel.*" *INST/TRANS, Internet-Zeitschrift fuer Kulturwissenschaften ISSN 1560-182X.*

Wien, Autriche. Nr. 16. 2006. <//www.inst.at/trans/16Nr/09_6/hanquart-turner16.htm>. Retrieved 28/09/2007.

3. Sudhir Kakar, *Intimate Relations: Exploring Indian Sexuality*, 2, 3.
4. Sudhir Kakar, *The Inner World*, 12.
5. Heinrich Zimmer, 148-51.
6. Salman Rushdie, *Midnight's Children* (1981; London: Pan Macmillan, 1982), 200.
7. Shashi Tharoor, *The Great Indian Novel* (New York: Arcade Publishing, Little, Brown, 1989), 18. Salman Rushdie, *Midnight's Children*, 38, 383, 384.
8. Sudhir Kakar, *Intimate Relations: Exploring Indian Sexuality*, 3.
9. Shashi Tharoor, *The Great Indian Novel*, 245. Salman Rushdie, *Midnight's Children*, 194, 256.
10. Shashi Tharoor, *The Great Indian Novel*, 245. Salman Rushdie, *Midnight's Children*, 194, 256.
11. Saiinan Rushdie, *Midnight's Children*, 148, 149, 176, 211, 463. Shashi Tharoor, *The Great Indian Novel*, 416-18.
12. Viney Kirpal, "An Overview of Indian English Fiction: 1920-1990s," Nilufer Bharucha and Vrinda Nabar, ed. *Mapping Cultural Spaces: Postcolonial Indian Literature in English* (New Delhi: Vision Books, 1998), XV.
13. Evelyne Hanquart-Turner, "Echoes, Palimpsests and Transmutations in Shashi Tharoor's *The Great Indian Novel*."
14. Salman Rushdie, *Midnight's Children*, 426. Shashi Tharoor, *The Great Indian Novel*, 418.

Select Bibliography

Balaswami, P. "'The Presence of the Past': Shashi Tharoor's *The Great Indian Novel* as Historiographic Metafiction." *Indian Literature Today*, ed. R.K. Dhawan, New Delhi: Prestige, 1994.

Choudhury, M.K. "The Eternal Present: Shashi Tharoor's Story of India." *Recent Indian Fiction*, ed. R.S. Pathak. New Delhi: Prestige, 1994.

Dhar, T.N "Entering History through the Backdoor with Tharoor and Vijayan." *History-Fiction Interface in Indian English Novel*. New Delhi: Prestige, 1999.

Karunakaran, Supriya. "Games the Novelists Play: The Subversive Rebellion of Vikram Seth in *The Golden Gate* and Shashi Tharoor in *The Great Indian Novel*." *Fiction of the Nineties*, ed. Veena Noble Dass and R.K. Dhawan. New Delhi: Prestige, 1994.

Khair, Tabish. "Shashi Tharoor." *A Companion to Indian English Fiction*, ed. Pier Paolo Piciucco. New Delhi: Atlantic, 2004.

Kirpal, Viney. "Politics and Philosophy in *The Great Indian Novel*. *Littcrit*, 16.1-2 (June-December 1990).

Narayan, Shyamala A. "Verbal Pyrotechnics: A Note on *The Great Indian Novel*." *Littcrit*, 16.1-2 (June-December 1990).

Rajan, P.K. "History and Myth in *The Great Indian Novel*." *Littcrit*, 16.1-2 (June-December 1990).

Ramakrishnan, E.V. "The Politics of Language and the Language of Politics." *Littcrit*, 16.1-2 (June-December 1990).

Shekhar, Sudhendu. "Shashi Tharoor: Adjuncts of History." *History and Fiction*. New Delhi: Prestige, 2004.

Tharoor, Shashi. "Myth, History and Fiction." *Seminar*, 384 (August 1991).

Tharoor, Shashi. "Yoking of Myth to History." *Littcrit*, 16.1-2 (June-December 1990).